Just For Tonight

KASSIA DEVANE

Contents

Chapter 1

SAVANNAH

The day had been a chaotic whirlwind; a relentless series of setbacks each adding to my growing pile of frustrations. This trip was supposed to be a kind of getaway for me, basically a working vacation; so far it was off to a rough start.

I'd been driving for just around four and a half hours and my kids had called me three times, each! At fifteen and sixteen, you would think they would be eager to get rid of mom for a few days, but no. Ever since my husband, Derek passed away three years ago, the boys took over the "man of the house" role.

My youngest, Chase, was cautious, sometimes to a fault. His last call was to be absolutely certain it would be okay if he used the money I left to order pizza for dinner. Which might have been a valid question had I not left it in an envelope marked *pizza money*.

Then again, it wasn't like I didn't know where he got it from. I'd called to verify the details of the author's conference twice. Same with the house I rented for the week. I cringed, remembering the irritation in the old man's voice. Did I sound that annoyed with Chase?

I shook off the comparison. This was my first vacation in, well, ever, and I was determined to relax. When I realized the weekly rate for this house was the same rate as four days at the hotel, I jumped at the chance to have a few days to myself, even if I would probably spend most of it prepping for the conference or working on my new book. I had the basic story down. I just couldn't seem to get the character profile for the male lead right. The details just felt off.

As I turned into the driveway, I was surprised to find a deep maroon pickup waiting for me. Taking out my phone, I double checked the date and address.

According to it, I was definitely in the right place.

A low rumble drew my eyes skyward just in time to see lightning race across the sky as a deafening crack rent the air. I slung my laptop bag over my shoulder and pulled my suitcase from the back seat, making a dash for the front porch.

The door swung open just as the toe of my boot kissed the first step. My body froze in place before the second shoe could land, as if some primal response had been triggered inside my body; I knew without knowing. I could feel the heat of his gaze burning through me before I lifted my eyes to meet his. Those green eyes I was certain I would never see again, not in this lifetime anyway.

My thoughts eddied, swirling away from me quicker than I could grasp them, slipping through my fingers as my mind emptied of all rational thought.

I put my foot down slowly, completing the step, steadying myself at the edge of the front porch. My mouth opened but refused to do more than quiver before closing again.

He wore the same confused look I was sure was painted all over my face, though, as usual, it looked better on him. He recovered quicker than I did, another thing that hadn't changed, his confusion melting into a lazy smile.

"Hey, Savvy. What brings you here?"

"Hayden." My tone more clipped than I intended.

I swallowed hard and tried again without the bitter edge. "I rented this house for the week. What, —, what brings you here?"

My throat clenched, holding my breath hostage as I waited for his answer. Truthfully, I didn't care why he was here, just how soon he would be leaving. He was my "never again is too soon" person. As in, if I never saw him again for the rest of my life, it would still be too soon.

His jaw tightened, the muscles in his throat becoming more prominent as he swallowed. "You must be mistaken, Savvy. I rented this place for the week."

Hayden and I pulled out our phones at the same time, both furiously pounding away on the keys.

"Hello."

"Hello, Mr. Calder, this is Savannah Kalen. I rented the house from you."

I pulled the phone from my ear and pressed the speaker button.

Hayden jammed his phone into the front pocket of his jeans and folded his arms across his chest.

"Oh, Kalen, yeah. I thought you already checked in," he mumbled. "Is something wrong with the house?"

"Mr. Calder, this is Hayden Young. I checked in with you about an hour ago, remember?"

"Yes, I remember," he answered, sounding confident for the first time since he answered.

Hayden faced me with a self-assured smirk. "See," he said, gesturing to the phone, as if those few words solved the issue entirely.

"Sir, this is Savannah Kalen. I spoke with you to confirm yesterday. I paid in advance. I have a receipt." I rattled off, pursing my lips.

"Yeah, Hayden. I heard you. What's this about?" he gruffed, clearly frustrated with the conversation.

"Well, you aren't the only one, buddy," I thought to myself.

"No sir. I said, Kalen, K-A-L-E-N," I enunciated the letters slowly, hoping it would sink in.

"Kalen," he murmured, his gravelly voice softening as he seemed to mull the words over. "Look, Kalen. My daughter will be here in the morning. I'll have her give you a call and straighten things out. Ok?"

A soft click and a dial tone sounded before I could open my mouth to speak.

"Son of a bitch!" Hayden swore from behind me, slamming the door shut.

"Not the way I was hoping to spend the night either," I shot back.

He snatched his keys from the sofa table, the metal scraping angrily across the glass as he dragged them to his hand. "Going to grab a bite to eat. I'll be back later, though," he called over his shoulder, not even having the nerve to face me.

"Nothing changes." I shook my head, barking out a mirthless laugh to the silent room.

Digging through my bag, I pulled out the can of chicken chowder. "Dinner for one." I sighed, pouring the soup into a small pot, the blue flames dancing to life as I spun the knob, flipping the gas burner on.

In the few short minutes it took me to heat the soup, the gentle tapping of the rain on the roof had turned into a cacophony of drum beats all playing different songs, no one note discernable anymore.

I set up my laptop at the kitchen table and pulled a bowl from the cabinet next to the sink. Once heated, I tipped the soup into the bowl, scraping the bottom of the pot to get every drop, then carefully put the heated bowl on the table.

I booted up my laptop and began ladling the chowder into my mouth. It was insanity to think either could distract my brain from thinking about Hayden. He still looked amazing after all this time. If anything, his body had filled out. He was still tall and lean, but there was a definition to his muscles that spoke of a quiet strength.

Once upon a time, he had been my best friend, a man I thought I might spend my life with. Damn, I had been naïve and stupid, just an idiot girl to think he wanted me that way. I swear if I lived to be seven hundred, I would never forget the look in his eyes when I told him I loved him. Nor could I forget the look he gave me in return, one that had seared into my memory. It wasn't the kind of moment a girl forgot...

It was hours later when the front door clicked closed quietly and the soft thudding of boots against the hardwood floor signaled Hayden's return. I kept my head down, mindlessly pounding away on the keys, the staccato rhythm tapping out a ridiculous scene I would no doubt need to cut during editing, but it kept my mind occupied for now.

"Can we talk?" he said, his tone much softer than I expected.

I looked up, trying to read the lines etched in his face, and nodded, pushing the keyboard away.

"What." I bit out. I may have cooled down some since earlier, but that didn't mean I actually wanted to talk to him.

"Look Savvy, would sharing this space be the worst thing in the world?" his piercing eyes had softened considerably since this afternoon.

"It's Savannah. No one calls me Savvy. Just you." I whispered the last words. No one had called me Savvy in seventeen years, not since him. I got the occasional Vanna, even a few Annas, even this one chick who tried making Vannahbelle a thing, but no one called me Savvy. I wouldn't let them.

"Ok, Savannah," he said, testing the name on his tongue. I'll be honest, I didn't like it. But I wasn't strong enough to hear the subtle caress in his voice as *Savvy* fell from his lips.

"I paid for the week. I need this place. Hell, the hotel hosting the conference is likely booked solid," I whined, hating to admit defeat, but the plain truth was, I had nowhere else to go.

"Jude died last week." His eyes slid shut, his chest rose and fell softly as he composed himself. Jude was his cousin. They were thick as thieves growing up, closer than most brothers. I had no doubt this was a devastating loss for him.

"My uh, my aunt said I could stay with them but- Sav- Savannah" -- he corrected himself, holding his hands up--"I can't be there. The pain, the pity, seeing them so broken, it takes my breath away." He pleaded, his voice thick with emotion. "I got this house so I could be there without actually being there, you know."

I nodded. Family ain't always easy.

"Look, Savannah, Jude's funeral is this week, and I have some family stuff. You have stuff too. Between the two, we should be able to stay out of each other's hair."

I was still not happy with Mr. Calder for double-booking us, but I had to admit he had a point. We both had plans for this week, and neither of us had better options.

"Despite our history, we're basically strangers. But I guess we can be reasonably certain neither of us is going to steal from the other and we're not going to murder each other in our sleep."

I tried putting a relatively positive spin on it, but something twisted in my gut at the thought of being this close to him for a week. I might be just some stupid girl he used to know, but he was my first love, and some wounds didn't heal.

Chapter 2

HAYDEN

I struggled to fall asleep, catching a few minutes here and there, ultimately, I tossed and turned until it was nearly five. The bed was comfortable, better than I expected when I booked the place, if I were to be honest.

No. It had been the look in Savvy's eyes. The subtle hint of fear that hid behind her timid smile. Sure, we hadn't left things in the best place, I could admit that, but fear?

The girl I had loved since I was fourteen was afraid... of me? I wracked my brain all night trying to come up with the answer, settling on the idea that Derek, the man she had chosen over me, must have planted it in her brain. There's no way the Savvy I knew, the girl I held when she broke her arm trying to impress me with a flip trick on my skateboard. Who stayed up all night holding my hand when I was cut from the basketball team. There was no way she would ever be afraid of me.

That sounded exactly like something he would have done. He was always jealous of the connection Savvy and I had and would have done anything to sabotage it.

I rolled out of bed, forcing my exhausted body through the motions of getting dressed and half-heartedly pulling the blankets over the bed.

"Time to make the coffee." I mumbled to myself, slipping on my boots and lumbering down the stairs, my footsteps heavier than I intended in the otherwise silent house.

I needn't have worried about waking Savvy. She was already up, sitting at the kitchen table, her laptop open, brows crinkled as she pounded away furiously at the keys.

"Morning Savannah." I called out, keeping my voice light.

She glanced up, her eyes flicking to the clock on the microwave.

"You're up early." she said, fighting back a yawn.

"My family has a tradition. When someone- dies," I swallowed hard, nearly choking at the mere thought of the word. "Everyone brings the family a meal and today's the day. You are supposed to present it to them with a fond memory you have of the person who has passed. Sort of helping to feed their body and spirit during this dark time."

"That's really beautiful," she answered softly. "So, you can cook now?"

A half laugh escaped my somber chest, "yeah. Us single guys gotta learn to cook if we don't want to starve."

"And here I thought you survived on beer and pizza rolls." She snapped back playfully.

"Don't knock beer and pizza rolls," I returned fire as I pulled the eggs, butter, shallots, mushrooms, and goat cheese from the fridge.

"So…" she said slowly, her brows crinkling as she took in the ingredients and utensils I gathered on the kitchen island. "Whatcha making?"

"Mushroom and goat cheese frittata." I said, picking up the knife and twirling it in my hand. "It was Jude's favorite. It's a small way to honor him. Sorta." I shrugged. "Hell, I don't know. It just felt like the right thing to make."

She hummed in agreement. "I'm sure Jude would appreciate the thought."

The wooden chair creaked as she stood, reaching her arms over her head and pushing herself up on her toes as she stretched. "It's about pumpkin time for me. I've been up all night trying to get this scene to work, and it still feels flat. Maybe after some sleep and a gallon of coffee, it'll fall into place."

She offered me a soft smile, but her eyes screamed with both exhaustion and the flood of unspoken words she held back. Sometime this week, when we're both not as tired and on edge, we would need to see about getting some of those words out.

I wasn't sure if it was possible to heal the rift between us. There are words you just can't take back and some wounds cut too deep, but for her, I would give it a shot.

I turned my attention back to my frittata, tossing the sliced mushrooms in the pan with the butter. A few clicks and the burner sprang to life. I stirred the buttery mushrooms and scraped in a thinly sliced shallot and went to work beating the eggs.

I worked quickly, putting together the frittata, my body on autopilot as my mind drifted to Savvy. She was the only person I had ever known who said, "pumpkin time". She was obsessed with Cinderella when we were kids. When it was time for bed, she would say "it's pumpkin time", as if her eight-year-old self might turn into a pumpkin like Cinderella's coach at midnight, if she didn't crawl into bed right then. Somehow, it just stuck.

My chest tightened, my heart trying to avoid that particular beat as I wondered, not for the first time, if she got her prince charming.

I knew she and Derek married. Of course, I knew they would from the moment I saw the rock he bought her. Our mutual friends tried to keep me in the loop for the first few months. Jude was the worst, but honestly, just the thought of her felt like razor blades against my already wounded heart.

He was a good man; at one time I considered him a friend. My only real complaint was that he wasn't me. But I guess I didn't really get to complain about that, now did I.

Hot air blasted my face, yanking me from my thoughts. I pulled the oven door down, shoved the pan in and set the timer.

I put on a pot of coffee and busied myself cleaning up the kitchen while the frittata baked, the savory aroma doing nothing for my roiling stomach. I had planned to fry a few pieces of bacon and an egg but opted for a few slices of dry toast instead.

After wrapping the dish tightly, I poured myself another cup for the road and slipped my jacket on, pausing midway when my eyes caught on Savvy's sleeping form. Her body draped across the sofa carelessly, as if she had fallen asleep as soon as her body touched the cushions.

Effortlessly beautiful, like always, her deep chestnut curls spilled over the pillow, framing the cheekbones I knew by heart and her soft lips that were gently parted, continuing down until the ends curled over the swell of her breast. Even after seventeen years, every inch of her was still pure perfection.

My stomach twisted as I watched her sleep, a flash of memories flooding back, tugging at old wounds I thought I'd buried.

I hadn't been able to take the time yesterday to really drink her in. Shock had sent us both running to our corners as the familiar fight-or-flight response kicked in. Even now I could feel the barrier between us, thick and strong like fortified steel. Somehow on the outside, I could only look through the tiny window I had been granted, my face pressed against the glass, greedily stealing glimpses of her, like a starving man feasting on the stolen images.

I finished sliding my arm into the sleeve of my coat, finally dragging my gaze from her and forcing my leaden feet toward the door.

Jude's death hit me so hard it knocked the breath from my lungs. I was still wheezing and gasping for air, nowhere near finding normal again. I certainly wasn't ready for God to throw her back into my life, shaking my world up like a snow globe. My emotions swirling around me like tiny bits of snow, certain that when the snow and glitter settled, I would be forever changed.

I balanced the coffee on top of the covered dish, holding it in place with my chin as I opened the front door and locked it behind me.

Today was going to be awful. The pained faces of my loved ones and the constant reminders of his absence. Hell, usually on a day like today, Jude and I would sneak away, only returning when our mothers noticed and chastised us for being disrespectful or unserious.

The stark realization settled on me as I closed the door and started my truck. As I pulled out of the driveway, Jude's absence was a raw, hollow ache, his memory filling every corner of the cab. Today was going to be hell.

Chapter 3

SAVANNAH

I woke just after noon, groggy and unsettled. Certainly not well rested, but I had already wasted too much of the day to sleep any longer. Today was meant to be preparation day. I had been asked to speak at a small writer's conference. It was a two-day event, showcasing some of the industry's most successful authors and me.

One of these things was not like the other. I frowned, self-doubt creeping back in.

My three novels had a small, loyal following, but mainstream success still felt out of reach.

My soft, fluffy romances under the pen name, Julie Blush, were garnering praise from a small group of readers, but I was having trouble moving beyond that to more mainstream success. In a word, I was stuck.

When they first offered me a spot, I was certain it was a mistake. Surely, they meant to offer the spot to someone with more experience. But the woman on the other end of the phone just laughed and said there had been no mistake.

I rolled off the sofa, clumsily righting myself, shaking off the remnants of sleep. Once the blankets were neatly folded and the sofa bore no signs I had slept there, I made my way into the kitchen and flipped on the coffee pot.

It was after dinner time and Hayden still hadn't returned. I spent the day memorizing my remarks for tomorrow and thinking up smart, pithy answers to what I assumed would be the most common questions. Basically, I had spent the day driving myself crazy.

I tried to write some, knowing my editor was expecting my next manuscript within a month's time and it was nowhere near completed. Instead, the empty page mocked me, my thoughts swirling too quickly to pluck one from the miasma and drop it onto the screen.

I told myself I was grateful for the quiet, but honestly, I would have preferred sparring with Hayden over wrestling with my imposter syndrome.

My phone chirped; saved by the bell, sorta.

"Hello," I said cautiously, hating that I had to answer unknown numbers this week.

"Ms. Kalen?" a sweet, sing-songy voice trilled out from the other side of the line.

"Yes."

"Hi, I'm Dana, Mr. Calder is my father." She started.

"Oh, yes. Thank you for getting back to me."

"Sorry it's so late. Dad actually wound up in the hospital this morning, and it was late before I got back to the house to sort through his things. "

"Oh, no! I'm so sorry to hear that." I sputtered. My heart twisted at the thought. Even if Mr. Calder was a stranger, I knew too well what it felt like to watch a loved one's health slip away.

"I see there was a mix-up. My father must have gotten your similar sounding names mixed up, Hayden-Kalen. I guess I can see it. He gets confused sometimes," she murmured that last bit. "I'm not sure exactly how to remedy the situation. Looking at the invoices, it looks like Mr. Young reserved the house first, but it looks like we received your payment first."

"Hayden- um, Mr. Young and I were actually childhood friends, but we sort of lost touch." That was close enough to the truth. I wasn't planning on baring my soul to a stranger.

"I'll be honest, staying here with him is- well, uncomfortable to say the least, but he and I have decided to give it a shot."

"Oh, that's great news," she said, releasing a heavy sigh. "I worked myself up in knots trying to figure out how to tell one of you to leave. I would like to apologize on behalf of my father. He was once a shrewd businessman, but old age, ya know?"

I nodded, shaking my head as I realized she couldn't see me. "Yes, I know. I went through something similar with my Gran."

"So, you two are all good then?" she asked, as if she sensed the agreement between Hayden and I might be more tenuous than I let on.

"Yeah, all good." I confirmed.

We said our goodbyes, and I cleaned up after the dinner mess.

I just returned to my seat at the table when Hayden strolled in, still cloaked in the heaviness of the day. He tossed his keys on the sofa table and trudged upstairs without a word or a glance in my direction, his footsteps sounding heavier with each step.

I began banging away at the keys, hoping my rambling thoughts and run-on sentences would somehow lead me to the missing piece of my story. I was vaguely aware of the shower turning on above me as I lost myself in the rhythmic tapping of the keys.

A warm hand landed on my shoulder, making me jump.

"Sorry. Didn't mean to scare you." He said, his voice was quiet as if he were afraid to scare the crazy lady in the kitchen.

"It's fine," I waved him off. "I just got used to the quiet house, and I wasn't expecting to hear a voice. That's all."

He looked me over from head to toe, his eyes finally settling back on my face.

"You look how I feel."

"That bad, huh?" I quipped, running my hand over my messy bun as I looked down at my ratty tee, trying not to be too sensitive about his obvious joke.

He chuckled dryly, "not what I meant. I was referring to the dark circles and the defeated look in your eyes."

"Oh, that." I said, making my voice sound light so he wouldn't look deeper. He always had x-ray vision when it came to me; he always saw too much.

"Wanna talk about it?"

I opened my mouth, a wicked reply on my tongue, but snapped it shut when my eyes found his. Pained, quiet desperation shone out, and I wondered to myself if maybe his offer was more about his need to vent and that still, small part of my traitorous heart wouldn't let me refuse him.

I nodded, waving my hand at the empty chair on my left. Instead, he tugged me from the chair, pulling me away from the table and the kitchen island to the space beneath the archway that separated the dining room from the living room. He wrapped me in his arms and began swaying.

"This isn't what I had in mind." I said, barely above a whisper, my pulse quickening at the familiar closeness of his body.

"You said talk. This is how we talk." He said with a careless shrug. His expression sobered, "Just for tonight Savannah."

I rolled my eyes but didn't argue. He was right, this was our thing, this was how we talked. Ever since the night my mom died when I was 13 and he snuck into my grandma's kitchen after everyone left for the night, this was how we talked.

I couldn't sit still, but I didn't know how to put my shattered thoughts into words, so he had held me, rocking me in his arms until nearly dawn. It had been the wee hours of the morning before I found my voice. Like my tears, once the first word slipped past my lips, the rest just seemed to pour out with no regard for my consent.

After that night, whenever one of us was having a particularly tough day, he would sneak in after his mom went to work for the night and we would dance in the kitchen and talk.

We swayed in silence, both lost in our own thoughts, the weight of his hand on my back, grounding me in this moment. Our bodies keeping time with music only we could hear, each of us releasing the occasional heavy sigh. Both seeming to fear breaking the silence in this quiet moment of our truce.

"My Aunt Gina fainted twice today. Twice." He said in a hoarse whisper, "I'm not sure she's gonna make it."

I nodded, remembering how hard my gran had taken my mom's death. Like Jude, my mom had been an only child. I was certain Gran only survived for me.

I hesitated. This was the part where I told Hayden all my troubles, but it didn't feel right. My problems felt silly next to his.

"Your turn Savannah," he said quietly, our bodies continuing to sway.

"It's silly." I started.

He shook his head, "not if it makes you look like this it isn't," he interrupted my protest.

I sighed, taking a moment to form my thoughts better. I already felt ridiculous comparing my insecurity to his grief.

"A few years ago, after Derek died, I started writing romance novels." I paused, waiting for the inevitable derision that came from people when I said 'romance', but it never came, so I continued. "I've been relatively successful, but I'm still nobody." I continued, fidgeting with the shoulder seam on his shirt.

"I got asked to speak at this writer's conference. Me. I was fine until I saw the final list of other speakers." I hesitated, swallowing hard. Did I really want to give voice to this fear? Was I comfortable baring my throat to him?

"They are all successful. Names I'd wager even you would recognize. Who am I to share a stage with them?"

He tipped my chin up, forcing my gaze to his. "You are Savannah Kalen. You are smart and strong and all around amazing and *they* are lucky to be sharing a stage with you."

If I hadn't been looking in his eyes, I might have let myself believe he was just bullshitting me, but the depth of his conviction that shone in his emerald depths, had me nodding along.

I forced a weak watery smile, hardly the picture of confidence.

"Are you planning to spend more time with your aunt and uncle? I'm sure they would love to have you around."

Hayden's mom worked nights, so Jude's parents took care of him during the day while she slept. They practically raised him.

He took my hand and spun me around, pulling me back into his arms, drawing a smile from me, a genuine one this time.

"I don't know what I'm gonna do. I just feel- helpless." He whispered.

I nodded. The words of comfort that once flowed so freely, stuck in my throat.

A comfortable silence settled between us, and I wondered if it was possible to extend our weeklong truce into the real world. Could I let go of my hurt feelings and my bruised ego? Could I have my best friend back?

I mulled the answers to those questions as we danced, slowly swaying as our feet carried us in the same small circle, retracing our steps over and over.

After what felt like hours, he pulled away, dropped a chaste kiss on my forehead, and turned and walked toward the stairs.

"Good night, Savvy," he whispered so softly I almost missed it over the hammering of my heart. "Night Hayden." I answered softly as I watched him climb the stairs to the loft bedroom, taking yet another piece of my heart with him.

Chapter 4

HAYDEN

Another restless night tossing in bed. Pretty sure this one was my own fault. What had I expected would happen after holding her in my arms?

One by one, memories danced through my mind like images from a projector I couldn't turn away from. The night her mom died, the night I was cut from the basketball team, the time her cat was sick, the first time we made love, my first time.

Hundreds of memories etched into my brain, woven so tightly into my being that not even these seventeen years apart could wrench them from me. I wasn't ashamed to admit I'd wept as the images paraded across my vision; my body still warm with the heat of hers.

I thought I'd known how everything would turn out. I was so sure, so blissfully, ignorantly sure. She and Derek had always been on-again, off-again, but I believed she'd come home to me in the end.

I was fine biding my time, til the day she came home with a ring, his ring. She didn't look happy. She looked small and broken; anguish painted across her beautiful features. Derek had thrown down the gauntlet, staking his claim, and now she would have to choose.

With her blank face, she held her left hand up for me to see. But it wasn't the sparkle of the diamond on her hand that caught my eye, but the tears gathering in the corners of her eyes. It didn't matter that she was at a loss for words, the slight wobble of her lip spoke for her. She couldn't choose.

So, I had done the only thing I could, the right thing, the stupid thing, the honorable thing. I slapped on the biggest smile I could muster and told her I was happy for her. It was the only time I had ever lied to her in the decade and a half I'd known her. Then, I'd shooed her away saying I had an imaginary date to get ready for.

I had known then I'd broken us, that the fracture was too deep for us to ever be right again, but if it eased her guilt, it would be worth it. I had never doubted my decision, never had regrets, until now. Until she stepped onto the front steps downstairs two days ago, looking like she was terrified -of me.

The soft thump of the front door closing rattled through the small house, the window behind the bed vibrating softly. That was my cue to get up.

Exhausted and devoid of sleep, I would have gone downstairs hours ago for coffee, but I couldn't bring myself to face her. I was a damn coward.

My boots thudded heavily as I lumbered down the steps, turning away from the sofa where she slept, where she insisted on sleeping, without even a glance and headed into the kitchen.

I flipped the switch on the coffee maker, the soft gurgle and the rich aroma lifting my brain from the mire before I'd taken my first sip.

The morning dawned overcast and colorless, as if the sky itself shared in my profound emptiness and couldn't muster up even the palest of blues to paint its wide expanse.

I settled at the end of the table. Not the end she used for her writing, not the sofa I was sure still carried her scent, and God knew I couldn't take another moment in bed thinking about her.

I winced as the wooden chair creaked and groaned as I dropped down a little harder than I intended, my coffee sloshing over the edge burning my fingertips.

"Dammit!" I swore, my voice loud in the silent house.

I swiped my arm across the table, my shirt soaking up the small amount of coffee that escaped my cup. My forearms braced against the edge of the table, both hands clasped tightly around the hot mug as I stared through the panes of the back door at the deep green of the tall pines against the colorless sky.

Robotically, I sipped the bitter brew, waiting for purpose and clarity, but nothing came. There was nothing to be done about this void between Savannah and me, not for now, at least.

There would be more family events this week. Tomorrow we would gather to hear Jude's Will read aloud. Later, there would be a wake, the funeral, and a general family get together the day after that. It would be amazing if we made it to the end of the week still speaking to each other.

But today was supposed to be a day to breathe before the chaos of the week set in. It was a nice idea in theory.

A book on the table caught my eye, a brunette with come-hither eyes gazing at a shirtless man in a tight pair of jeans. I stifled an eye roll.

"Lost Days, by Julie Blush," I read the title aloud. "I wonder if this is the kind of thing Savvy writes?"

The chair creaked as I leaned back, flipping the book open to the first page.

Hours later, Savvy stormed in, rattling the windows in their frames as she slammed the heavy wooden door.

She froze when she saw me, her eyes wide, her mouth opening and closing like a fish on a riverbank. She dumped her things unceremoniously on the floor next to the sofa and rushed to the bathroom, slamming the door behind her.

I heard the shower turn on and I turned back to the book. There were only a few pages left before the ending.

It was nearly an hour later when Savvy came out of the bathroom, steam billowing behind her, her hair soaked and her skin bright red as if she'd just come from a long day at the beach.

Her eyes scanned the room, almost as if she was assessing the small space for hidden threats. When they finally landed on me, she swallowed hard, not quite able to meet my gaze.

"What's wrong?" I asked, hoping last night had built enough good will that my question wouldn't earn me a "fuck off" in response.

"Nothing. It—it's nothing. Long day." She sighed, waving off my concern.

I had spent the previous and all day feeling like a lost puppy, desperate for clarity, but as I took in her haggard form, I knew what I needed to do.

Before I could think, my hand reached for hers, the movement so natural it felt like muscle memory. I pulled her close, her warmth flooding the empty spaces in my chest as we began to sway. Every step was familiar, a rhythm we hadn't shared in years but hadn't forgotten.

"Talk to me," I said quietly.

Her feet kept up with mine as we shuffled in a slow circle, but her body remained rigid and unyielding, her face tight as she stared unseeing at my chest.

I had given up on her talking, deciding I would be content to just hold her for however long she allowed it, when she finally spoke.

"Just for tonight." Her voice quivered, but her body relaxed in my arms.

"Just for tonight." I echoed, nodding my assent.

She rested her cheek against my chest, my arms wrapped around her, pulling her closer.

"Eliza Priddy," she murmured.

"Eliza's pretty?"

"No," she answered, a half-smile finding its way to those soft, perfect lips. She smacked my chest playfully. "Priddy, with a *d*, well, two of them. She's an author, like me, only she has a bigger following than I do. Our readers go back and forth razzing each other, a harmless rivalry. Anyway, she was at the writer's conference today and—"

She shook her head, her dark curls bouncing as her face rubbed gently against the waffle-knit of my shirt. Her eyes flicked up and found mine, and she offered me another half-smile.

"Sorry, I had a crap-tastic day. Somehow, the slides for my speech got out of order. I'm sure you can guess the rest. I got flustered, I stuttered —and Eliza, she —she folded her arms over her chest and smirked at me."

"I was angry with myself for the mix-up. I wished the ground would open up and swallow me right then and there so I wouldn't have to endure the weight of the pity in their stares. But that smirk—God, that smirk—it set something off in me. The whole point of the conference was to support each other, wasn't it? And yet, there she was, acting like she'd won something.

"I barely remember the rest of the day," she admitted, tears gathering in the corner of her eyes, but refusing to fall. "How am I supposed to face them tomorrow?"

With that watery admission, her entire body deflated, melting against mine as we continued tracing circles across the hardwood floor.

I knew holding her again would wreck me, just like it had the previous night, but I couldn't bring myself to care. She needed me and I would be here until she sent me away.

A soft laugh rippled through her, finally bringing a smile to her face. "I called her every name I could think of, you know, in my head. I finished my speech with a smile pasted on my face, but in my head..." She shook her head softly, her voice trailing off.

"Do you think she sabotaged you? Messed with your slides?"

Her shoulder lifted in a half-hearted shrug. "At first, I thought it was a mistake, then -that smirk. If you had asked then, I would have said yes, but now- now I'm not so sure."

"Want me to kick her butt?" I asked, falling into that familiar role.

"No." she snorted. "This isn't eighth grade, and she's not the school bully. I'll have you know I solve my problems like an adult these days."

"So, that's what, red wine and chicken strips?" I tossed back at her with a playful smirk.

Her mouth dropped open, and she placed her hand delicately on her chest. "Are you saying there's something wrong with red wine and chicken strips?"

"Oh no, milady," I said, pulling back just enough to offer a mocking bow. "I would never question your culinary choices, even if dino nuggets are the superior choice," I retorted, my face twisted in a mask of mock sophistication.

She broke first. A loud boisterous laugh burst from her chest, bouncing off every surface, banishing the solemn mood that had settled in the tiny house.

My own laugh answered hers seconds later and for just a few moments, the heaviness lifted. Not just the tension of the day, but the entire morass of unspoken words and unfulfilled promise that hung between us, smothering what was once a bright flame.

The smiles slowly slid from our faces as reality trickled back in, the spell of the moment broken, but still, we continued to sway, clinging to each other.

"I've missed this," I breathed.

"You'v—You—" her mouth gaped open, and though the words abandoned her, the accompanying emotions written on her face were the same ones that echoed through me: pain, regret, longing.

"I—I think it's time for bed." She managed, placing her palm against my chest and pushing away gently, a chill sweeping in where her warmth had been only a moment ago.

Her eyes searched mine for a few more heartbeats before she turned away, wordlessly crossing the small distance to the sofa and began spreading out her bedding, effectively dismissing me.

"Good night, Savannah," I said quietly.

She mumbled something I thought might have been good night as I trudged up the stairs, my footsteps as heavy as the heart in my chest, sinking lower as if pulled downstairs by some unseen magnetic force.

Any other night, I might have listened to the skittering of my heart and gone back to plead with her—to figure this out and finally make things right, or at least as right as things between us could ever be.

I slid into bed, the chill of the sheets magnified by the memory of her warmth and the aching loss of it.

Tomorrow, my family would gather for the reading of Jude's Will. They were mostly good people, but stress and grief did strange things to people. I needed to be in the best frame of mind for the coming week, and yet, I couldn't pass up the chance to fix what I had broken all those years ago.

I drifted into a fitful sleep with both Jude and Savvy swirling in my mind, two kinds of grief, both powerful and all-consuming. My mind was so full and heavy I almost missed the soft sniffle that drifted up to the open loft bedroom where I lay—a final stab in my heart as sleep finally claimed me.

Chapter 5

SAVANNAH

I hardly got any sleep last night. Every time I got close, another wave of memories crashed over me and the cycle started all over. "He misses this." The unmitigated gall of *him* to say that to *me*.

It took two extra cups of coffee before I felt ready to face day two of the conference, but as I stepped into the chilly room, all thoughts of exes, rejections, and midnight confessions fled my mind. I slipped into my avatar's persona.

Savannah Kalen might have needed to worry about those things, but Julie Blush did not.

I set my notecards and macchiato next to the marker bearing my name and surveyed the room as it quickly filled with eager young authors, all hoping to glean some information from the conference that might give them an edge.

That morning there was to be a short workshop: *How to Structure Your Story to Keep Readers Hooked.* After lunch, there was a Q&A session where the attendees could ask questions of the speakers. At the end of the week, there would be a reader appreciation event. That was the part I was most excited about.

I found Eliza Priddy in the crowd and flashed her my biggest fake-it-till-you-make-it smile and offered a friendly wave. Her Cheshire cat grin slid off her lips as I turned away, shaking off yesterday's disaster, focusing on enjoying the rest of the conference.

It was late afternoon when the door finally clicked shut behind me, sealing away the world beyond these four walls. Hayden wasn't back yet. I knew he had something today, but I hadn't asked. I meant to, but when he told me he missed dancing with me, all my rational thoughts and intentions fled, my mind bombarded with flashes of his rejection. How the fuck could he say he missed me when he was the reason we weren't together?

I shook my head, trying to rid myself of the unwanted thoughts, the questions I wasn't sure I wanted answered.

I set down the bag, pulling out the plastic containers that held my salad and chicken parm. The day had gone well, really well if I were to be honest, but I was still too exhausted to bother cooking tonight. I promised myself I would make something extra healthy tomorrow night.

I opened my laptop and dug in. Maybe I could get a bit more written tonight before bed. Oddly enough, the random scenes I had pounded out while trying to avoid thinking about Hayden led my story in a new direction, breathing new life into a book I was struggling to finish.

The door snicked closed quietly, and my every thought evaporated as I took in Hayden's haggard form.

His hair was tousled, as if he'd spent hours running his hands through it. But it was his eyes that really froze me to the core, devoid of light and humor. The whites of his eyes, now painted an angry red, were the only signs of life I could find in them.

I rose from the chair, hastily closing my laptop and rushed to meet him, my hesitations completely forgotten as I met him at the foot of the stairs.

He dragged his gaze to mine, emotion igniting in his emerald depths-. I fought the urge to shudder as his icy hand cupped my cheek. A pained smile shattering the illusion of him, the jagged pieces falling like shards from a broken mirror revealing the broken man within.

My heart clenched as pieces of the wall I built between us, pieces we had been slowly chipping away at the last few days, finally gave way.

I knew that face, and it sent a pang through my chest. It was the same one I'd seen in my mirror after Derek died—vacant and lost. Two weeks after the accident, I had caught my reflection and barely recognized myself. The way my clothes hung haphazardly from my body and the tangled mess of hair in desperate need of a good washing was bad enough, but it was the empty, vacant look in my eyes that shook me. A look Hayden now wore, only thinly veiled by a smile that didn't quite reach his eyes.

He moved to the side, stepping around me. "Night, Savannah," he said with a tight whisper.

I lurched forward, bracing my palms on his forearms. "Are you okay?" Fuck! That's a stupid question. "Have you eaten?" Mildly better, but I'll take it.

He shook his head. "No, but I'm fine." His half-smile lied as he continued trudging up the stairs.

In a daze, I walked back to the kitchen, my gut twisting when my eyes landed on the container of chicken parm. Memories assailed me from those dark days after my husband's death. I was lucky there had been people who cared enough to make sure my kids, and I ate. It was a kindness I could do for Hayden.

I laughed to myself at the irony. I hadn't wanted to cook and had ended up ordering take out. Now, here I was making him dinner, God did have a sense of humor.

I pulled open the fridge, the chilly air waking me from my momentary stupor. My eyes jumped from one container to the next, taking silent inventory. A leftover chicken breast from my last night's dinner and bacon from his breakfast this morning, looked like a good place to start.

The shower flipped on overhead, and I sighed in relief, knowing it would buy me a few extra minutes to prepare something.

The cutting board slammed into the counter with a heavy thud after the corner slipped from my shaking fingers.

I slid the chef's knife out of the block, cut the bacon slices in half and thinly sliced the chicken breast.

Another quick trip to the fridge and I grabbed the onion and tomato I had already sliced for my salads, a head of romaine, mayo, and ranch dressing. My arms were loaded, but I managed to snag the loaf of bread between two fingers as I carried everything over to the cutting board.

I toasted two slices of sourdough and slathered on equal parts mayo and ranch, then topped them with the chicken, bacon, lettuce, onion, and tomatoes. I cut the sandwich diagonally, then stood back to admire my handiwork.

I grimaced at the sheer size of the behemoth, ultimately shrugging it off. If there was anyone whose big mouth could handle that monstrosity, it would be Hayden.

I released a heavy breath and then another, steeling my heart for what it might find at the top of the stairs.

By the time I reached the stairs, I had worked myself into a steady rhythm and was feeling more confident. A little more confident, maybe, ok, well that part was a lie, but I was doing my best.

Just as I reached the top and stepped into the loft bedroom, the bathroom door opened. Hayden stood there in only a too small towel, wrapped dangerously low on his hips. Steam billowed all around him, like the big reveal in an old sci-fi movie.

Our eyes met, and my confidence abandoned me. "I made you dinner," I said, my voice sounding small to my ears.

"Thanks," he said, taking the plate from my hand and dropping to the foot of the bed, quickly devouring the sandwich and setting the plate aside.

I stood there, a silent observer, unsure if I was even wanted in this moment, but desperate to do anything to alleviate his anguish.

"Is there anything I can do?" I asked quietly.

His eyes slowly rose to meet mine, but he said nothing.

"Do you want to talk?" I tried again, holding my hand out, reaching for his.

He stood slowly, his eyes never leaving mine, and crossed the small space between us.

Instead of taking my hand, he brought his up to cup my cheek, his thumb tugging gently at my lips.

"This isn't a dance in the kitchen night, Savannah," He said in a hoarse whisper. "You should probably go downstairs."

The air between us felt charged, humming with tension; that familiar electricity began building quickly between us, my heart thundering in anticipation.

"I'm not going anywhere." I placed my palms against his chest and whispered the familiar refrain: "Just for tonight."

Chapter 6

SAVANNAH

"I'm not going anywhere." I placed my palms against his chest and whispered the familiar refrain, "just for tonight."

He leaned in slowly, giving me plenty of chances to pull away, but I had no intention of backing out now.

His lips ghosted across mine, the barest whisper of a kiss.

"Last chance Savannah," he whispered against my lips.

I pushed back slightly until our eyes met. "I'm not going anywhere," I repeated, my voice firm and clear.

I snaked my arms around his neck and pulled him down to me.

Our lips met in a maelstrom of heat and electricity, decades of pent-up emotions colliding with the raw heat of our blatant desire.

We clung to each other, his fingertips digging into my skin and gripping me tighter with every slide of his tongue against mine.

He pulled away just long enough to tug my shirt over my head.

I gasped, every inch of my body electrified as he trailed wet kisses down the column of my throat, dragging his tongue back up before biting playfully on my ear.

His hands slipped around, expertly unhooking my bra as his lips trailed lower, his tongue tracing a fiery path across my shoulder and down to my nipple.

His tongue swirled around the hardened peak before he sealed his lips around my nipple and sucked.

Lightning zinged through my veins, a sharp jolt spearing straight to my clit.

My back arched, pressing me further into him, tearing a wanton moan from me.

His other hand swept over the heated flesh of my bare stomach, reaching up to squeeze my other breast, pinching my nipple gently.

He dropped to his knees, dragging his hands down my sides, his possessive grip making my pussy throb. The sight of him kneeling before me, his eyes hungry, almost desperate as he worked to rid me of my pants, cracked something open in me.

I stepped out of them, and he wasted no time leaning in and placing a kiss against the thin cotton barrier separating him from my pussy. I flinched, all at once becoming self-conscious. Why didn't I change out of my mom panties?

I squeezed my thighs together, my hand darting down to cover the offending lilac cotton. "I'm sorry. I—I didn't really prepare for this. I didn't shave. I'm wearing these—" I rambled, my anxiety ratcheting higher with each intrusive thought.

"Savvy," he interrupted, his voice strained, earnestly pleading, "do you want me?"

I nodded, "God, yes." I whispered. "But-"

His hands that had been resting on my hips gripped the band of my panties and slid them down. "You didn't shave before our first time, either" he said matter-of-factly. "And I enjoyed the fuck out of that."

"Ok, but-"

My words were cut off as his tongue swiped across my lips, my legs parting, eagerly seeking more contact and a deep moan spilled from my lips.

I pushed away, running my fingers through his silky curls, my legs shaking like a newborn fawn as I crawled onto the bed. His eyes traced my every move, a predator stalking his prey.

My heart thundered as I adjusted myself on the bed, allowing my legs to fall open, a thrill racing through my blood when his lips parted as he took me in, spread out before him.

I crooked my finger, beckoning him forward, releasing him from the invisible chains that bound him.

He crawled up the bed slowly, my hips squirming in response to his predatory gaze. He hooked his arms under my thighs and with a final smirk; he licked me from my opening up to my clit, his tongue flicking over the sensitive bud rapidly, causing my legs to shake.

My hands fisted in his hair, pulling him closer as my hips rocked in desperate jagged waves chasing my release.

"Oh God. Oh. Oh fuck," I whimpered, my head thrashing as my orgasm slammed into me, taking my breath away.

He lapped up my release greedily, his teeth grazing my overstimulated clit, beginning the climb toward my next release.

I tugged gently on his hair, and he crawled up my body, leaving a trail of hot kisses in his wake. "Still fucking delicious." He murmured.

Before his words could penetrate the haze of orgasm, his lips slammed into mine. I gasped. His tongue swept in, dancing with mine, making promises our bodies were certain to keep.

The head of his cock notched at my entrance. He pulled away and studied my face, needing reassurance, and my heart melted just a little more.

I nodded, smiling softly as I brought his lips back to mine in a tender kiss.

He thrust in, filling me in one go. His body shook above me, a deep groan vibrating through him as he stilled, burying his face in my neck.

"Fuck Savvy! You feel so good." He choked out in a hoarse whisper.

After giving us both a few moments to adjust, he began moving, finding his rhythm at an almost brutal pace. He continued his passionate assault on my mouth. I tried to keep up with him, his cock had me gasping and moaning, giving him better access as he plundered my mouth, but left me unable to focus on kissing him back.

Every touch of his hands was a white-hot brand, every thrust a claim. This wasn't a teenage boy fumbling through making love to me, through our first time. No, this was a man who knew exactly what he wanted; me.

He reached between our bodies, rubbing furious circles over my clit as he fucked me harder still.

The heat building in my core was unbearable. Yet my hips squirmed, needing more.

Stars burst behind my eyes, that pool of warmth now a tsunami engulfing my entire body, waves of pleasure crashing over me, crashing into each other and taking my body to new heights.

He froze, only kissing my lips softly as my body quivered and the euphoria slowly subsided.

"That's exactly how I remembered it," he rasped.

"What?"

"How exquisite you are when you come. The look in your eyes, the way you feel clenched around me—it's pure perfection."

" He pressed his lips to mine and resumed thrusting, this time in slow, languid strokes.

I gasped, my body quivering at every brush of my overly sensitive skin.

"I'm not done." He whispered; his eyes locked onto mine.

I nodded, pulling him down into a slow, passionate kiss, as I raised my hips to meet his every stroke. He cupped my cheek, cradling my face in his hand, emotion burning brightly in his emerald eyes. Still, he said nothing as we moved together.

After what felt like hours of intense, intimate lovemaking, he buried his face in my hair and thrust harder and faster as he chased his release.

I locked my legs around him, pulling him impossibly closer, digging my nails into his lower back as my own pleasure crested the wave. A hard pinch on my clit pushed me over. My body froze as the entire world shrunk to just that moment, then shattered into a billion pieces.

"Hayden! Uh—I—nnnngh—uh." A string of unintelligible sounds rushed out of me as I came.

God, I love you. I thought to myself. I know it makes me an idiot, but I still love you.

He stilled above me, my name a whisper on his lips as he released himself deep inside me.

We laid there tangled in the sheets, trading soft kisses and gentle touches, neither of us willing to break whatever spell brought us to this moment.

Finally, he sighed, "I need a shower. Want to take one with me?"

I shook my head.

"Ok. I'll be back soon." He dropped a kiss on my nose and got out of bed, his god-like muscles flexing with each movement held my attention until the bathroom door closed.

I left the bed and headed downstairs. The smart thing would have been to join Hayden in the shower and spend the night in his arms. That's what he was offering, right?

But I just couldn't.

I stepped into the downstairs bathroom and flipped the shower on. As I waited for the water to heat, I stared at my reflection, unsure what I was searching for but certain I didn't see it.

I climbed into the shower, pulled the curtain closed behind me, and leaned against the wall. The cold tile was jarring against my still heated skin, but I welcomed the shock.

I slid down the wall, allowing the heated spray to wash over me, hot tears pouring from my eyes and blending with the water swirling down the drain.

"What have I done?"

Chapter 7

HAYDEN

Yesterday was brutal.

Jude called me out from beyond the grave. Even as the attorney reading Jude's Will aloud spoke, I heard the admonishment in Jude's voice. "You had the love of your life in your hand, and you sent her away. And your stubborn heart refuses to open for anyone else. You fucked up, man. Fix it."

"Let my death be your reminder: life is short. Go find Savvy. Pour your heart out to her. Grovel. Do whatever you need to, so that when you face the end of your days, you won't have these regrets."

I climbed into the cab of my truck, heaving a heavy sigh as the engine roared to life. Today was Jude's funeral, it would take nearly a half hour to get to my aunt's house and it would take every second of that to calm my raging heart.

Jude's words played on repeat as I eased out of the driveway and turned onto the tree-lined street, along with flashes of Savvy writhing beneath me, moaning my name. I could still feel the sting of her nails digging into my flesh as she shattered in my arms.

My emotions had been so raw, my thoughts so muddled, I couldn't get the words out. I offered her an out. I told her to go, but she stood firm; a solid rock against the storm of me.

A sacrificial lamb. Beautiful and pure. Perfect and at least for last night, mine.

"God, I love you," She had whispered, her eyes glassy and unfocused, still lost in the post orgasmic haze. I still wasn't sure she knew she had uttered those four life-changing words out loud.

It was enough to give my weary heart hope. I knew that hope could be dangerous, but for the moment, it was all I had. I wasn't one of those 'love conquers all' people. There were still miles of pain between Savvy and me and no matter how much I wanted it to; I was certain a hot night between the sheets wouldn't fix it.

Hope and grief and uncertainty warred within me the whole drive, making it impossible to clear my mind. I didn't want to show up to Jude's funeral with my mind resembling three-year-old Savvy's first attempt at fingerpainting. Jude deserved better than that. Or did he? It was his words that whipped my thoughts into a frenzied hurricane. Not that he could have possibly known I would go home to her after hearing those words.

I pulled into the driveway and shut the engine off. The silence was jarring set against the competing voices in my head and the thundering of my heart.

The ride out to the cemetery was rough. Mom asked me to drive while she and Uncle Tommy sat on either side of Aunt Gina, holding her as she sobbed. Occasionally, she would let loose a soul rending wail, an unearthly sound I knew instinctively would haunt me the rest of my days.

Jude had insisted on a graveside service and asked people to refrain from bringing flowers, maintaining that if they wanted to spend money on him, they should have taken him out for a burger and a beer while he was still alive.

Still, dozens of arrangements were placed behind his casket, a beautiful contrast to the cold metal of the casket and the still colder grave beneath.

The service was a blur. I barely remembered walking to the small dais, and I swear, even with a gun to my head, I couldn't have told you what I said.

It must have been good since there wasn't a dry eye in attendance.

Aunt Gina wrapped me in a bone-crushing hug, weeping harder, murmuring how it wasn't fair for God to separate her boys and lamenting how this was the last time the warm rays of the sun would kiss his face.

By the time I got back to the house, I was wrung out, emotionally empty. Hollow. I would almost rather spend the night in my truck than face Savvy.

I stepped through the doorway into the darkened house, closing the door behind me softly so as not to disturb her.

I toed off my boots, in hopes of remaining silent.

The light clicked on softly, and I sucked in a shuddering breath when my eyes fell on Savvy, curled up on the sofa with her feet tucked under her. Her chocolate waves had been tamed into a messy top knot, but it was her reddened cheeks and her tear-stained face that caused my heart to stutter.

I stumbled forward, my legs moving with no regard for my wishes. Every cell had only one goal: dry Savvy's tears.

My eyes never left hers as I lowered myself to the sofa, the empty cushion between us felt like miles instead of inches.

She regarded me silently, her eyes sweeping over me until they settled back on my face as she stood, swallowing hard. "We should talk." She said, holding her hand out for me to take.

I wrapped her dainty hand in mine, my thumb caressing the back of her hand. Was she really asking me to dance?

I stood and offered her a half-smile. I wanted to beam down at her, radiating happiness like her own personal sun. But the half-smile was all I had left in me, my own light snuffed out. Smothered by the pain and grief of seeing my loved ones so broken.

She led me over to the space beneath the archway, her socked feet sliding over the hardwood as she shuffled along. Her arms wrapped around me, heaving a deep sigh as she laid her head against my chest.

"Jude's funeral was today." I started the conversation as we began to sway.

"I had no idea. I'm so sorry about Jude." She murmured into my shirt. I knew they weren't just empty words to her; she grew up right alongside us and I had no doubt she felt his loss too. "I can imagine how hard today must have been for you."

My throat knotted and I couldn't speak, so I just nodded and squeezed her a little tighter.

"Do you wanna talk?" she asked, her brows pinched tightly, concern painting her delicate features.

"This is the place for it." she said, cutting her eyes toward our makeshift dance floor and offering me a half smile.

"One day." I said, giving my head a hard shake. "I don't have the words right now, Savvy. But one day." I finished resting my forehead against hers.

"It's ok. You don't have to say anything if it's too hard. I'm here." she breathed, reaching up to brush away tears I hadn't realized were falling again.

I pulled her closer, wrapping my arms around her more tightly, greedily soaking in the comfort of her body in my arms. Jude would love this moment and hate it. He would love seeing Savvy and I reunited, but hate that we were spending a minute of our precious time talking about him.

I took a deep breath, hoping to change the subject. "Your turn." I whispered, stroking her cheek with the back of my hand, wishing I could wipe away her obvious pain.

She shook her head softly, "we don't have to get into it tonight."

"Uh-uh." I said, lifting her eyes to mine. "That's not how this works. I showed you mine, now you show me yours." I replied, both of us offering a halfhearted chuckle at my lame attempt to add some humor to the moment.

Her fingers clutched at the heavy fabric of my shirt as she sucked in a deep breath. "I spent the day arguing with myself."

"Well, I hope you won." I quipped.

She snorted, shaking her head softly. "I haven't actually decided which part of me won."

"You wanna talk about it?" I nearly choked on the question but forced the words out. "Does it have anything to do with why you didn't stay with me last night?"

She pulled her head away enough to look into my eyes but stayed pressed against me and nodded.

She released her lip from between her teeth, slowly dragging in a long breath. "I just needed some time to process. I wasn't–"

"You weren't ready." I finished for her.

"No! Well, yes -but." She groaned in frustration, "No, I wasn't ready. But I didn't know I wasn't ready. Shit. This is not coming out right."

"Just slow down," I said quietly, rubbing large circles over her back. "Try again."

She froze, her body no longer swaying with mine.

I hooked my finger under her chin, lifting her eyes to mine.

Her watery eyes were bright with emotion, her lip quivering as she tried—and failed—to get the words out.

She shook her head, as if she could shake away the pain and anguish that held her voice prisoner. "Last night- was the first night, my first time since–" She took a few deep breaths, her shuddering exhale evening out after the third or fourth one. "Since Derek died." She finished, her voice barely above a whisper.

I stilled, shock and confusion stampeding through my head making me wonder if I should drop my hands or pull her closer.

"It's been a while since–"

"Three years," she supplied. "Derek died three years ago, last March."

"And you've been alone all this time?" I couldn't hide the disbelief that seeped into my voice.

She sighed, closing her eyes. "There is so much we need to talk about. Conversations I don't think either of us have the energy or the mental capacity for, not tonight. Can we just pretend that everything is good between us; like it used to be?" she implored. Her eyes opening to reveal my own pain and exhaustion mirrored back at me. "Just for tonight." Her hushed request whispered like a prayer for mercy.

I leaned down, pulling her closer, pressing a lingering kiss to her lips. Fuck yes, I wanted this woman, but I couldn't bring myself to repeat the lie anymore. I didn't want her 'just for tonight', I wanted her for the rest of my life and even though she wasn't ready to hear it, the thought of saying otherwise made me feel dirty.

Instead, I kissed her tenderly, whispering against her lips. "Spend the night with me." My hands slid down her arms until only our fingertips connected us.

She looked up, tossing me a bashful half-smile and nodded.

My heart thundered as I led her up the stairs and tucked her into bed next to me. Both of us were too tired for sex, but deeply craving an intimate connection. I groaned at the perfect feel of her naked body pressed against mine.

I only had minutes to enjoy the feel of her in my arms before sleep overtook me. I welcomed it, tiny rays of hope dancing at the edges of my consciousness.

Chapter 8

I woke wrapped in Hayden's arms; my body caged against the familiar wall of muscle. His breath heated my neck and shoulder, sending pulses of warmth racing straight to my core, shocks of electricity laced with anticipation—even though he wasn't even awake yet.

I closed my eyes, focusing on my breath, but that only seemed to make it worse. With my sight gone, my focus shrank down to the feel of his heated skin against mine and the way our bodies rose and fell together rhythmically with each breath.

My eyes flew open. Nope, this was not working. I moved to get up, but his strong arms coiled tighter around me.

"Stay in bed, Savvy," he groaned, his voice thick and gravelly. "It's too early to get up."

I relaxed against him, giving up my half-hearted attempt at leaving the bed. I had no real desire to leave his arms, anyway.

"We should—" his lips ghosted across the skin just behind my ear, and my thoughts evaporated like raindrops in the summer heat.

"I -I um." Another wet kiss as his hand glided down the plane of my stomach, teasing my hip crease.

"Breakfast, we—" another half-hearted protest escaped me.

"Mmmm" he groaned, his voice rumbling in his chest. "Breakfast sounds amazing."

He nipped my ear, his finger tracing lazily along my slit.

I let my legs fall open, turning in his arms.

"Good morning, Savvy." He whispered against my lips.

"Good morning yourself, handsome." I answered, his tongue sweeping in to steal my breathy reply.

He traced a hot path down my throat and across my collarbone. His tongue flicking across my nipples, hardening them into stiff peaks before sucking one into his mouth and sucking hard.

My toes curled and my back arched off the bed, pressing me against the steel frame of his body.

"Hayden." I whispered, somewhere between a plea and a command.

I couldn't put into words what I was feeling or even what I needed, but he seemed to know.

He raised his eyes to mine and pulled his finger to his lips, licking it slowly as his green eyes bored into mine. His hand slid under the covers, shivers racing through my body as it ghosted down my stomach.

The wet tip of his finger stroked over my clit, pulling a deep moan from me, tempting my soul to leave my body.

He flashed me a wicked smile, fully aware of the effect he was having on my body as he continued kissing down my body.

By the time he reached my pussy my body was wound tight, like a bowstring, ready to be set off with the slightest of touches. My breath came in short, frenzied pants, each one a whispered cry for release.

I cried out as his tongue replaced his finger. "Oh, God yes!"

His fingers teased over my body until they found my nipples. He pinched and twisted them as he circled my clit with his tongue, flicking it and sucking it into his mouth.

My hands twisted in his hair, holding him against me as I pushed myself further into his mouth.

"Fu- Uh- Fu-oh! Hayden!" I screamed his name, losing control as my orgasm hit me like a tidal wave.

He lifted his eyes to meet mine, licking his lips, like an obscene tiger savoring his meal.

I dropped my head back against the pillow, trying to slow my racing heart and quivering thighs. Anything to keep him from seeing how deeply his every touch affected me.

"Just sit Savvy," he said, flipping a towel over his shoulder as he slid the bacon into the pan. Barefoot and bare chested, the epitome of a domestic god standing barely five feet away.

"I told you I would make you breakfast this morning," he said with a cocky smirk.

I snorted, "I didn't think you would actually remember saying it. I figured you were too wiped out."

He nodded, moving the bacon around in the pan. "I was, but I will never break a promise to you."

Well, thanks for leaving the door wide open. I blew out a long breath, hoping to steady my voice. "So, you wanna talk about it?" I asked.

"Do you?" he tossed back.

"No." I laughed, "not really. But I guess we should."

"The day before yesterday was the reading of Jude's will." He said quietly. "Jude's last words for me, his last wish, was for me to find you" He laughed, raising his eyes to the ceiling and giving his head a soft shake. "Of course, he couldn't have known I would leave that moment and come directly to you."

"It's funny how life works sometimes." I offered.

He nodded, "anyway, he wanted me to find you and say some things. Words I never had the courage to say back in the day. And I'll be honest, I'm not sure you're ready to hear them yet."

I ground my teeth together, biting back my acerbic reply. I wasn't ready, I scoffed internally. He was so full of shit. Except... except for the fact that I wasn't ready to see him again. Wasn't ready to dance with him again. And I certainly wasn't ready for his lips to crash into mine and go tumbling into bed with him. God, anyone but him.

As much as I wanted to argue, I understood where he was coming from, so I nodded wordlessly.

"Last night, when I told you I wasn't ready when we slept together, I-"

"I know. I understand and listen Savvy," he said, not giving me a chance to finish my thought. "I wasn't thinking this morning. I wanted to taste you so fucking bad. All I could think of was getting my head between your thighs. I'm sorry if I crossed a line but I swear I won't fuck you again until you ask me for it."

"If! If!" he interjected, holding his hands up like he was trying to placate an angry cat. "If you ask me. I'm not making any assumptions, I swear."

I shook my head but couldn't contain the sardonic laugh that bubbled out of me. Could he really be that thick?

His eyes snapped to mine, studying me with that gaze that always saw too much but somehow not enough at the same time. He slid a plate of bacon on the counter between us and cracked a few eggs into the pan, yanking his hand back quickly when the bacon grease spattered.

"Did I say something wrong?" he asked.

My mouth opened and closed, trying to find the words to avoid this conversation, my heart desperate to skip the beats that were sure to follow.

I cleared my throat and tried again, my voice coming out barely above a whisper. "I wasn't ready, but- How do I explain this?"

"Just spit the words out, Savvy," he said, sliding the eggs onto the plate with the bacon and flipping the burner off. "You can always rearrange them if they don't come out the way you want."

He walked around the counter, coming to stand in front of me. "I was your best friend once upon a time. You know I won't twist your words. Just say whatever you need to."

I nodded. He was right. I knew he would listen until I got my words across, but this time, that was the problem.

"If I had spent the night with anyone else, it would have hurt afterward, but with you." I choked down the emotion, rising in my throat, threatening to cut off my voice altogether. Even now as I wrestled with the guilt, my body still ached for it to happen again. "With you, it felt like a betrayal of my vows *because* it was you."

Please don't make me say it. Please don't make me say it. Please don-

"I'm sorry Savvy. I don't understand." He held his hand out, "Let's have a proper talk."

He pulled me into our spot beneath the archway, wrapped me in his arms and began to sway, waiting for me to continue. But the words thickened in my throat, refusing to pass my lips. So, I remained silent in his arms.

If I lived to be a hundred, I would never understand how this man, who was usually so observant, couldn't see the woman in love with him—even when she was in his arms.

Chapter 9

HAYDEN

We danced, turning in circles over the same small area of hardwood. The same way we danced around the unspoken words between us. "Not ready." What an asshole comment. Savvy was stronger than I was, and here I was, treating her like an emotional teenager. The truth was, I was too afraid to say those words.

I thought giving her up would spare her pain, but all it did was shatter both of us. And now, all I could do was stand here and watch the love of my life fall apart again—because of me.

"Look, Savvy," I started, dragging in a deep breath. "We both have things we need to say—things it might feel easier to keep inside."

She nodded but kept her eyes on the floor, the opposite of what I was going for here.

I tipped her chin up, finally bringing her eyes to mine. My thumb ghosted softly across her cheek. "The girl I found on the front steps a few days ago, the one who paled at the sight of me is somehow the same girl who tumbled into my bed the other night and the girl who still melts in my arms every time we dance. Somehow, those are all the same incredible person."

"Talk to me Savvy," I murmured.

Her lip quivered, but she didn't look away. "You go first." She challenged. That was Savvy, always challenging me.

"Ok," I nodded, huffing out a hard breath. "Jude told me to find you and tell you—I love you, Savvy. I always have."

"You- you love me?" she whispered, stepping backward out of my arms.

"You. Love me?" She said again, her voice stronger this time.

I stepped forward, and she raised her hand between us.

"You loved me so much you rejected me," she said in a strangled whisper.

"Savvy, I-"

"I came to you with my heart in my hand and my clothes on the floor," She gritted out.

"And his ring."

"What?" she whispered, her tear-filled eyes snapping up to meet mine once again.

"Your heart in your hand, your clothes on the floor—and his ring on your hand. That's how you came to me, Savvy.

Her hand flew to her lips, and she shook her head, her tears now falling freely. Another step back and she turned, my hand closing around her arm before she could get another inch further away.

"Don't do it, Savvy," I rasped out, not afraid to beg. "Don't run away."

She turned to face me, her eyes like fractured sapphires, hardened, but beautiful. "I'm not running, Hayden—I'm walking," she said, flinging her arms out, then letting them slowly drop.

"Like I should have done the minute I saw you." She shook her head, her mouth twisted in that scowl I knew meant nothing good for us.

A humorless laugh bubbled up through her, spilling from her lips as she spoke. "You love me? You destroyed me," she finished through clenched teeth.

"Savvy." I pleaded.

"Don't call me that." She ground out, ripping her arm from my grasp.

"No!" I called out, anger lacing my voice. "You don't get to just decide for us."

She whirled around to face me, nearly crashing into me as I followed her into the living room.

"No. That's you that makes the decisions for us then. Huh?"

"Yes, I did." I stepped back, pushing out a heavy breath before continuing more softly. "You looked so torn. Like having to choose between us was ripping you to pieces-"

I stepped forward, cupping her face. I knew I was only getting one shot at this. I needed to say everything in my heart and not hold anything back. "When I walked into my room that day, it was like my wildest dreams and my worst nightmare collided right in front of me. The woman I loved, the girl of my dreams, had come to me, offering herself to me. It was the best moment of my life." I whispered, unable to stifle the soft smile that rose on my lips at the memory.

My hands slipped down her arms, pulling her fingers up to my lips, dropping a kiss where her wedding ring used to sit. "Then my eye caught the sparkle, and I remembered he'd proposed."

"You knew? How?" she asked, her tear-filled eyes blown wide in horror.

I barked out a hearty laugh. "How do you think I knew? The bastard told me himself. Make no mistake, Savvy, he was staking his claim on you. He couldn't have made that clearer if he'd pissed on your leg."

That earned me a laugh, well, more of a snort, but she smiled, so, I would take it.

"I didn't know he told you. I-I just didn't think."

"We were both in love with the same girl," I said softly, brushing her hair back from her eyes and tucking it behind her ear, the stubborn strand slipping back to cover her eye. "You didn't know how I felt, but he could tell. He knew."

"We were so young, Savvy, I thought we had time." My eyes slid shut, unable to bear the weight of this moment. "So stupid." I whispered.

"So, when you told me you didn't want me- you were what, being noble? Is that it?"

"Something like that." I answered quietly.

"You think you were being noble? You didn't take the burden away—you just left me alone with it.

"I thought you were confused. That maybe, you really did feel something for me, and you couldn't choose between us." I sighed heavily through my nose. "I wish you could have seen yourself the way I saw you. You looked like you were being crushed under the weight of the choice. So, I took away that burden."

"That simple."

"It was anything but simple. Trust me on that one Savvy. I gave up the one thing I wanted the most."

"You were right." She nodded, swallowing hard, "I was torn that day. I thought I was happy until he put that damned ring on my finger.

I smiled, threw myself in his arms, all the things a happy girl in love would do."

She dragged in a shaky breath, her head falling back to stare at the ceiling.

I stayed silent, needing to hear her side of things as much as she needed to release the words.

"Once I got home and crawled into bed, once it was just me alone with my heart, all I could think about was how that stupid ring changed everything. It cost me you.

Her eyes dropped to mine, her tears again flowing freely. "I wished you had been the one to give me that ring."

She stepped forward until her toes pushed against mine and whispered so low I could barely hear the words. "That's why I came to you. I came to ask you if you felt something for me. If maybe we could try having something real."

"You married him." I choked out. That was the short answer. Regardless of what happened between us, she had married him.

"I married him because I couldn't have you," she shot back.

My heart that had been thundering since I opened my eyes this morning, knowing this conversation had to come, stuttered, skipping several painful beats as she confirmed what I had known all along. Every ounce of the searing pain and loneliness I had lived with for the last seventeen years was my fault.

Chapter 10

"I married him because I couldn't have you." The words slipped out, shocking us both into silence.

Of course, the truth wasn't quite that cut and dry, but it was close. Hayden's brows disappeared into his perfectly tousled hair. My stomach clenched as I remembered the reason his hair was mussed was because he'd spent the morning between my legs.

I swallowed hard, my mouth opening and closing, trying to find the right words to

explain.

"Fuck! Why is this so hard?" I yelled, running my fingers through my hair, tugging at the roots.

"Talk to me, Savvy. Just spit it out. We'll find the right words together, OK?"

I stepped backward, but Hayden pulled me back into his arms and began to sway.

"Please, just talk," he whispered into my hair.

I leaned back, searching his eyes. We were already chest deep in this conversation; far too late to gloss over the past and pretend nothing happened. Our pain and secrets were already strewn across the floor like discarded broken toys that nobody wanted to claim anymore. So, what's one more admission?

"I was in love with you both," I started, a mirthless laugh spilling from my lips. "You've gathered that much by now, for sure."

He nodded, his face expressionless as he listened to me without judgment, just like the old days.

"I guess I didn't understand what I felt for you until the thoughts of losing you came raining down on me. I spent all night imagining different scenarios, my life with each of you, knowing choosing one would cost me the other." I shook my head, desperate to clear the images from my mind.

"Imagining life without Derek hurt. It was difficult and painful to think of losing him. But imagining life without you took my breath away. We were occasionally lovers, but you were so much more than that: my best friend. My sounding board. The person who knew my every secret. All but one." My shaky voice was barely above a whisper as I admitted the truth I kept locked away these long years.

His eyes slid shut, his forehead dropping to mine as we continued to sway, our steps tracing over the same small circle.

I wished he would say something. Call me names. Take back his declaration of love. Anything. But true to form, he remained silent.

"I came to you." I tried again, "A-and then you sent me away. You slammed that door in my face, so I grieved the loss of you and threw everything I had into loving Derek."

"And you were happy," he said quietly. "You were happy with him."

"Yeah, for almost fourteen years we were happy." I hummed in agreement. "I never said I didn't love him or that we weren't happy."

I caressed his face, his green eyes opening to meet mine, my voice cracking as I whispered my plea for understanding. "I meant that if I had the choice between the two of you, I would have chosen you."

He nodded, dragging my fingertips up to his lips and kissing them softly.

"Jude was the one who told me when Derek died. He pushed me to go see you. He said you needed comfort, but I—" He threw his head back, swallowing hard as his confession got caught in his throat. "I told myself you wouldn't want to see me. That me showing up would do more harm than good."

He flashed me a sad smile, shaking his head slowly. "The truth is, I was a damn coward. I was too afraid to face you."

Hysterical laughter bubbled up through my lips, shattering the somber mood.

"Fuck, we're both bad at this," I managed to eke out between bursts of laughter.

Hayden threw his head back, his answering laugh harmonizing with mine, ricocheting off the walls instantly lightening the heaviness between us.

For a moment, the years of pain and regret melted away, leaving only two people laughing like kids again. The sound was foreign but so welcome, like sunlight breaking through storm clouds.

"We may be bad at this, but we could have been so good together." He whispered, his voice low and gravely, sounding almost pained.

"Yeah, we could have." I answered softly.

"It's not too late, Savvy." His eyes searched mine, the emerald green catching the early afternoon sun, pouring droplets of gold into those endless pools I would gladly drown in.

"We can't go back and recapture those years, but we could start over from right now."

"Like, wipe the slate clean? Erase everything?" I asked, an edge of hurt and confusion seeping into my tone.

"More like, forgive each other for the mistakes we both made. Fuck, Savvy, we were kids," He replied, running his hands through his hair, pulling on the ends as he released a frustrated sigh. I couldn't help but remember the feel of those hands in my hair.

I wanted to forgive, even if I could never forget. I just didn't know if I had it in me.

"Can we just put a pin in this?" I said, my shoulders dropping as my entire being deflated, the will to argue abandoning me completely. "Just for tonight."

His eyes softened, his head bobbing in agreement. "Yeah, just for tonight."

He pressed his lips to mine, his lingering kiss, a promise to make everything right between us again. The thing is, I wasn't even sure if that was possible.

I pushed aside the fear and doubt that threatened to crush me. Those could wait until tomorrow. One last reprieve, the calm before the storm.

He offered his hand to me, and I took it like the lifeline it was, offering him a tentative smile in return. No, things weren't settled between us. Hell, if anything, things were messier than they had been at the start of the week.

"So, how do you want to spend the afternoon?" he said, wiggling his eyebrows and tossing me a cocky smile.

"Down boy," I said, shoving him playfully. "There will be plenty of time for that later."

"So, does that mean you'll spend the night with me?" he asked, wrapping his arms around my waist and pulling me flush against his body.

In that moment, I couldn't bring myself to utter the snarky response that had been on the verge of escaping my lips, as I took in the sincere, almost pleading look in his eyes.

"Yes." I breathed. "I'll spend these next two nights with you."

There were only two nights left. After that, we would go our separate ways, back to our lives and the real world. The very least I could do was spend these two nights in his arms. Sunday morning was rapidly approaching, and if I'd learned one thing these past seventeen years, it was this: time marches on.

It didn't stop just because I wasn't ready for it to move forward. It didn't stop when Hayden rejected me, leaving me to pick up the broken pieces of my heart and glue them back together. And it certainly didn't stop when that eighteen-wheeler crossed the center line and took my husband's life, shattering my world into a billion pieces.

Nope, it just kept pushing along, and I knew this would be the same. No matter how much I wasn't ready for this week to end, it would. And because God had a sense of humor, it would arrive with beautiful blue skies, rainbows, and fluffy clouds to mock me.

I pulled him over to the sofa, dragging him down on the plush cushion next to me and pointed to the large flat screen that hung over the crackling fireplace.

"Put something on."

"Any preferences?" he asked, reaching for the remote.

"Surprise me," I said, tucking my legs under me and leaning my head on his shoulder. "Nothing gory. I'm not feeling up to watching anything bloody."

He hummed in agreement, the sound vibrating through the air as he dropped a gentle kiss on the top of my head, then started flipping through the available shows.

Our time together was quickly coming to an end, and I yearned to savor every precious moment with him, creating memories that would forever hold a special place in my heart.

Chapter 11

HAYDEN

Savvy reached for the remote, pausing the movie. The actors on screen froze in amusing positions neither of us bothered to notice. Their plotlines forgotten the moment her lips touched mine.

A deep groan rumbled through my chest as she crawled into my lap, her knees digging into the cushions as she pressed her body into mine.

Her lips were soft and enticing as she nipped playfully at my mouth and chin, cupping my face with both hands.

I kissed her back gently, allowing her to take the lead. Not that it was really possible to stop Savvy from taking what she wanted.

Her tongue thrust into my mouth, sliding against mine. Her head bobbing up and down as she sucked my tongue, and my cock hardened painfully in response.

Fuck, I loved this woman.

Soft, whimpering moans slipped from her as she ground herself against my erection, and I greedily swallowed every sound.

My heart raced as my hands slipped under her shirt, a thrill of heat and anticipation shooting through me, my fingers aching to touch the soft, velvety skin that embraced her curves.

"I want you." I whispered against her lips.

Her eyes slid shut as my hands slipped down to hold her hips in place as I pushed up into her.

This was my idea of beauty: Savvy with her head thrown back, eyes closed, lips parted, lost in her desire.

Her gaze dropped to mine, something snapped between us, neither of us holding back or bothering to pretend we didn't want fuck more than we wanted to breathe.

I lifted her shirt, and she quickly squirmed out of it.

Her fingers, usually so steady and sure, fumbled with the button on my jeans as her movements became frantic.

"Ugggh!" she growled in frustration, yanking on the waistband. "Get these off."

I pushed her off my lap, ripping at the button and yanking down the zipper. "Strip." I commanded, her body jumping to obey.

I lifted my hips, sliding my jeans down and freeing my aching cock, giving it a few languid strokes while I waited for her to finish.

"Come here," I whispered, my voice low and gravely as I reached for her hips, pulling her down across my lap.

Our lips crashed together, the heat of her mouth only fueling my desire, ratcheting it up notch after fiery notch. My hands tangled in her hair, twisting until she whimpered, her lip quivering as I swallowed the delicious sound.

Her hips rocked forward, desperate for friction. My own hips jutted upward in response, my dick pushing through her slit, finding her already wet for me.

She wrapped her hand around my cock, giving it a firm squeeze as she lined it up with her entrance.

Her hands pressed against my chest, the tips of her fingers curling under as she pressed herself down with a hiss.

"Fuck, Savvy. Fuck, baby you feel good." I groaned.

In one motion she dropped onto my lap, fully seating herself. Her head dropped back, pushing her breast into my face.

"Hayden." She whispered my name like it was her favorite prayer, her nails digging into my skin as she raised and lowered herself slowly a few times before picking up the pace, riding me hard.

I tried sucking on her nipple, but her frantic pace made it hard to keep it in my mouth. I palmed both breasts, squeezing gently as my lips found their way to her neck, trailing sloppy kisses along the column of her throat. Sucking hard when I found the spot that elicited a sinful moan that went straight to my cock.

I pulled her up, standing and twisting us around. With a growl, I tapped the back of her thighs, and she climbed onto the sofa, resting her forearms on the back. She yelped as I planted my foot on the sofa, grabbing her hips and ramming back into her. Her head dropped to the sofa with a whimper as I fucked into her hard.

She rocked back into me, trying to meet me thrust for thrust, but the punishing rhythm I set kept her nearly pinned in place.

I wrapped her chocolate curls around my hand, twisting and pulling until her head snapped back up with a gasp. Her thighs shook as I pounded into her; I could tell she was close. Me too, Savvy. Me too.

My hand snaked around and rubbed furious circles over her clit.

"Hay-Hayd-uh-nnnnguh" she moaned, her voice a string of unintelligible sounds as she came undone, her release triggering my own.

I released her hair, and we both dropped to the sofa, completely spent.

"I love you," I whispered against her hair. Now that the dam had broken, the words flowed effortlessly.

Pulling the threadbare rust-colored chenille throw from the back of the sofa, I wrapped it around us. She nuzzled against me, her nose brushing my neck, and her palm pressed lightly against my chest, her fingers tracing lazy circles on my skin.

As I held her in my arms, my chest still heaving, the weight of what we'd shared—and what still hung between us—settled heavily in the air. I knew the conversation wasn't over, but for now, I just wanted to hold her.

"I love you too, Hayden. I always have." She murmured.

I ran my fingers through her damp hair, something in the tone of her voice made my gut twist, a cold shiver of unease dropping into my stomach like a stone in a lake.

"Savvy, I-"

"Can we not?" She interrupted, lifting her eyes to mine. "I know we still have a conversation to finish but," she sighed heavily, "can we just not ruin this beautiful moment? Can't we just put it off-just for tonight?" she whispered the magic words that had carried us through this week.

Every cell in my body screamed how important it was to finish this now, to rip the band-aid off. We had already laid everything bare, hadn't we? What else could be lurking unseen in the shadows waiting to pounce?

But as I looked up into those bright blue eyes, heavy with exhaustion, my head nodded of its own accord. I just didn't have it in me to deny her. Especially not now after the emotionally taxing day we had.

We were both exhausted, but it wasn't just from the day. It was the weight of all the words we hadn't said, the years of silence that stretched between us. I wanted to take that burden from her, but I didn't know how.

I released a heavy breath and changed the subject. "So, what do you want to do for dinner?"

She smiled. It was only a half-smile, but gratitude and relief shone in her vivid blue eyes.

"How about pizza?" she suggested.

I nodded. "You still a freak who likes pineapple on your pizza?" I asked, arching my brow and tossing her a wry smirk.

"Um, yeah. It's delicious and let's not forget you're a freak too. Only you add jalapenos to your ham and pineapple." She shot back, her smile widening.

I pulled out my phone and scrolled through a listing of the local pizza joints, punching in a quick delivery order.

"Garlic knots or cheesy bread?" I asked.

She scoffed, "is that a real question?"

"Both." I mumbled completing the order.

"It's going to be nearly an hour until the food gets here."

"Good," she said, wrapping her arm around me and placing her head over my heart. "I am in no hurry to leave this spot."

I guess that's what it all boiled down to in the end. For Savvy, moving on from this moment meant watching this week fade away in the rearview mirror as she drove back to her life. Me, on the other hand, I was hoping this was the beginning of our fresh start.

I know I really fucked up seventeen years ago. I just hoped I could get Savvy to give me a chance to prove how good we could be together.

I knew she was counting the hours until this week was over, but I was counting the hours until I'd lose her again. The thought of watching her walk away was unbearable, but I didn't know how to stop her.

Chapter 12

SAVANNAH

The heaviness in my eyelids warred with the incessant chirping of my phone, dragging me down as I pleaded for five more blissful minutes of sleep wrapped in the warm cocoon of Hayden's arms.

My fingertips danced along the edge of the nightstand, searching futilely for the source of the offending noise. We must have knocked it off last night.

There was a moment last night when Hayden was slamming me into the headboard so hard, I would swear the entire house was shaking, no doubt the nightstand got jostled during our passionate encounter.

"Good morning, Savvy," Hayden whispered, his voice thick and heavy with sleep.

He pulled me closer, rolling on top of me, pressing his lips to mine as his arm fished around off the side of the bed, pulling my phone up just as the shrill tone sounded once again.

"Thank you." I whispered, taking the phone from him and silencing the alarm.

He took my phone, dropping it on the bed as he settled himself between my legs. Need pulsating through me as his cock pushed through my slit, the head teasing against my clit as he made slow circles with his hips.

"Good morning to you too." I giggled, tracing my fingers down the side of his face. God, he really was a beautiful man.

His tongue traced along the seam of my lips, and they eagerly opened for him. My tongue darting out to welcome his.

The kiss was tender and unhurried as if we could both spend all day in this very spot chasing our pleasure.

Of course, that wasn't close to being true, and even as he licked a fiery trail down my throat, nibbling on that spot that made my toes curl and my clothes fall off, I knew we had to put on the brakes.

"Hayden," I whispered, my voice fluttering as my skin heated in response to his touch.

"Mmmm." He answered, his mind clearly focused on the task at hand.

"I-I have to—fuck." An arrow of pleasure shot straight to my clit, completely wiping all thoughts from my mind.

I cupped the back of his head, pulling him closer and tried again.

"H-Hayden. I-uh, I need to get ready."

"Mmm. Ready." He groaned against my ear, his heated breath, drifting over my skin making silent promises I longed to let him fulfill, but I had to grab a shower and get dressed and-.

He pushed into me with one long roll of his hips. A deep groan rumbling through his chest as he bottomed out.

"Fuck." I moaned. "Who needs breakfast?"

His lips found mine, and they tangled in a heated frenzy, our tongues mimicking the slide of our bodies against each other.

I cried out as the first wave of pleasure crashed into me. Hayden didn't slow his pace, his hips snapping hard and fast as he worked me toward my second peak.

"Fuck, Savvy!" he growled, sweat beading on his forehead.

He snaked his hand between our bodies, his thumb rubbing frantic circles over my clit.

"Come with me, Savvy."

The pleading in his voice was my undoing, the need so raw and pure.

I threw my head back and whimpered as the sensations overwhelmed me, my throat quivering as I struggled to find my voice.

"Hay-oh- I- uhh! Oh! Fuck!" I sang my incoherent song of pleasure as tiny jolts of pleasure zinged through my body like lightning in my veins.

He dropped his forehead to mine and whispered, "I could get used to waking up like that,' he said, his lips curling into a lazy, satisfied smile.

The smile that lit his face tugged at my heart, twisting and wrenching, it threatened to pull it from my chest.

I didn't want to ruin this beautiful moment, and we didn't have time for this conversation right now, hell, I was going to be late as it was. All I could do was offer him a smile. At least, I hoped it was a smile.

His touch set my skin ablaze, but I couldn't stop the small voice in my head whispering about the cost of giving in. Did I dare let myself dream about a future with Hayden, or was I setting myself up for heartbreak all over again?

"I need to get ready." I said, barely above a whisper.

"I know." He said, throwing me a lazy smile. "That's why I'm not joining you in the shower."

I pushed against his chest playfully. "You're terrible."

"You didn't seem to think so a minute ago." he said, throwing his head back shaking with laughter.

"Ha ha. You're hilarious. Now, move your sexy ass. I gotta go." I said, pushing against his chest again. This time his body easily tipped over onto his side allowing me to crawl out of bed.

I slipped down the stairs naked, my feet barely kissing each step as I rushed to get ready. Each step making me question whether I was rushing toward my reader event, or was I rushing to get away from the man who made my heart beat faster with both fear and excitement?

The door to the bathroom snicked shut quietly, leaving me alone with the hot water and my racing thoughts. "*I don't have time for this,*" I chided myself.

There were times I hated being right, and this was one of them. Hayden felt amazing this morning, but it cost me. I was running nearly twenty minutes behind schedule; it looked like I was going to have to forgo breakfast and coffee. Actually, I was sure the event coordinator would have coffee on site, but breakfast, yeah, I was outta luck on that one.

I stepped out of the bathroom, hopping on one foot as I tugged my boots on. My eyes flicked up and landed on Hayden wearing a cocky smile and a pair of gray sweats slung low on his hips, one foot propping the front door open.

"Your breakfast, Madame." He said, holding out a plate and a coffee mug.

"Is that a-?"

"A fried egg sandwich. Yep. Hope you still like those."

I nodded, "yeah. Love them."

He passed the plate and coffee to me, dropping a lingering kiss on my lips before stepping out of my way.

"Knock 'em dead, Savvy."

Exactly one hour and ten minutes later I was just putting out the last of the merchandise I'd brought with me as the first of the readers trickled in. I dropped into my seat and took a sip of the bitter potion he prepared me, creamy, but not quite as sweet as I usually liked it.

"Ugh! I loved this one." A small woman with large brunette ringlets gushed, picking up a copy of my first book, *Awkward Nights*.

"Do you mind if I ask you a question?" she leaned in, whispering conspiratorially.

"No, go ahead." I said, slipping into my Julie Blush persona.

"Where on Earth did you find the inspiration for Jameson Parker?" she bit her lip, her brown eyes sparkling with excitement as she waited for an answer.

The answer was simple, Hayden. He and Derek had been sliced and diced and bits of their physical and personality traits carefully stitched together to form all my male characters, even the assholes. But I had come up with the idea for Jameson after having a particularly vivid dream about Hayden, so that character was all him.

I threw out a couple of filler sentences while my brain worked. I wasn't sure I wanted to bare such a personal part of me to a stranger.

Finally, I settled on the truth. "He's actually based on my first love."

"Oh! Did you hear that?" the woman said, one hand flying up to cover her mouth, the other over her heart. "Her first love."

She laid the copy down, grabbing the matching character art and bookmark. "Can you please sign it to Zoey?" she asked, digging in her bag and eventually pulling out her card.

"Sure Zoey. I can do that." I said, flashing her a smile.

"My first love was an asshat." A woman said, coming up to stand next to Zoey. "Only good thing that man ever gave me is that little girl." She said, waving her hand in the direction of a small child with bright blue eyes and long blonde pigtails.

"She's beautiful." I said, offering her a genuine smile.

She nodded. "Thank you. For her, I would do it all over again though. Ya know?"

"My first love was really great," Zoey said, color blooming on her cheeks. "I was the idiot who messed it up."

I placed my hand over hers, "Same. My first love was an incredible man, and I was too stupid to see it until it was too late."

With that began an entire day of telling tales of my and Hayden's friendship and budding romance. It seemed that every story grew the crowd by at least one or two more people. Some listened, and some shared their own stories, while others offered advice.

I signed dozens of books, completely selling out of Awkward Nights and I signed until it felt like my hand might fall off.

All in all, a good day.

My phone chirped in my bag, followed by another, then another in rapid succession. Somehow my phone had made its way to the very bottom, but I finally pulled it out, my face breaking into a smile.

Both of my boys were texting in our group chat.

Max: Hey mom. Just wanted to check in.

Chase: Hey Mom. Excited to see you tomorrow.

My heart skipped several beats, and I quickly pounded out replies to both of them.

Max: Everything is fine here. Stop worrying.

I wasn't -ok, fine. I backspaced away my worried message, settling instead on something more upbeat.

Chase: You are coming home tomorrow, right?

Max: Chase and I are making dinner. You'll be home by six, right?

Me: OMG I miss you both so much.

Me: Of course I will be home tomorrow by six.

Max: Ok. I know you have your meet and greet or whatever today. Have fun. LU.

Chase: LU2 Momma.

Me: I love you both. See you tomorrow.

The warm feeling washing over me turned icy between heartbeats. The sweet messages were a stark reminder of the roadblocks ahead. No matter how much my heart ached for Hayden, my boys were my world. Every decision I made, every risk I took—it all came back to them. And I wasn't sure how Hayden fit into that world, or if he could and Max and Chase would always come first.

Chapter 13

HAYDEN

I slammed the door a little harder than I intended. Dropping my head back against the headrest, I let my eyes slide shut. Today hadn't gone well.

At Jude's funeral a few days ago, Aunt Gina had been an absolute wreck, crying and wailing until she passed out twice. Uncle Tommy and Mom had literally held her upright at times. It had been hard to watch.

Today she was all smiles and sweet, sing—songy voices. At every mention of Jude, her spine went rigid, and her face froze in place— an iron mask willing away all emotion.

If it weren't for the slight wobble of her lip and the glassy sheen of tears too stubborn to fall, I might have thought she was doing better.

But witnessing her "I'm fine. Nothing to see here" act, was brutal.

Everything else was fine. Brunch was fine. Uncle Tommy was fine. I mean, he looked like a grieving human being, but at least it felt real.

Every time Mom caught me staring, she shot me a look that was loud and clear: drop it.

I hadn't even had the heart to share that I found Savvy, and we were reconnecting after all these years apart. At least, I hoped that's where this was heading.

The truth was, the memory of falling asleep and waking with her in my arms had given me strength, far more than she would ever know. She was the reason I hadn't broken completely.

I could see the hesitation in her eyes, and I knew despite every misunderstanding we had cleared up, every secret laid bare, there was still an immovable wall between us, something she was still unwilling to tear down and fully let me in.

This wasn't just about tonight. It couldn't be. Every time she smiled at me, I felt like I was holding on to something ephemeral, something that might vanish by morning if I didn't find a way to make her stay.

To make matters worse, we were running out of time, running out of *just one more nights*. Hell, we hadn't even exchanged phone numbers. If we don't get things figured out, and soon, it could be another seventeen years before we find each other again.

With a quick turn of the key, the truck roared to life. I backed out of the driveway, aiming for that tiny house with the loft bedroom, where I got to sleep holding the love of my life, at least for tonight.

It was nearly seven when the headlights from Savvy's car flashed across the living room wall, signaling her return.

I hadn't asked her how late she would be tonight, so I had to look up the event to see what time it ended. Luckily, there was only one conference in town this week that had anything to do with books.

My timing was a little off, and the food had been sitting for about fifteen minutes. I hoped it wasn't too cold. No, steak needed to rest before cutting. I didn't misjudge the timing; I was letting the steak rest. Sure. That sounded convincing.

Savvy danced through the door, popping it closed with her boot. Her brilliant blue eyes dimmed slightly as they met mine, but she recovered quickly, offering me a soft smile.

At second glance, I noticed the way she slouched, as if her skin were almost just hanging off her bones and the tinge of exhaustion behind her smile.

"Dinner's ready," I said, pretending not to notice her change in demeanor. Her grateful smile confirmed it had been the right move.

She walked toward the kitchen, unceremoniously dumping her laptop, purse, and whatever else she was carrying onto the sofa.

"Smells amazing," she said, stepping into my open arms and nuzzling her face against my chest.

Savvy let out a soft laugh, but it didn't quite reach her eyes. Her hand lingered on my chest for a second longer than necessary, as though she was grounding herself in the moment before it slipped away.

I held her tightly, my face buried in her hair as I breathed her in, silently vowing this would not be our last night together. We still needed to finish our talk, and I would do everything in my power to convince her to give me one more chance.

She pressed her hand to my chest, pulling away gently. "So, you said there's food. Cause I'm starving." she said, her wide eyes imploring me to feed her.

With one arm still wrapped around her, I reached down and tore off a piece of sourdough bread, dragging it through the olive oil and herbs before lifting it to her lips.

She opened wide, taking the bread and most of my fingers into her mouth, moaning as she licked my fingers clean.

My cock throbbed hard, instantly jealous of my fingers.

She flashed me a wicked smile, stepping around me and taking a seat at the table.

"Holy crap! That's a lot of food. It's just the two of us, right?" she asked, taking in the dinner I cooked to impress her; steak, Brussels sprouts with bacon and feta cheese, fettuccini Alfredo, and sourdough bread.

I sighed, dropping into my chair opposite her. "I only have one more night to get this right. So, we have food," I said, waving my hand across the prepared dishes.

"Dancing," I nodded toward our makeshift dance floor.

"And if those don't get the job done, we can go upstairs." I said, waggling my eyebrows suggestively.

She burst out laughing, her hand flying up to cover her mouth. "You've got all the bases covered, huh?"

"I hope so," I said quietly, dipping some of the Brussels sprouts onto my plate and drizzling some balsamic vinegar over them. "It's shaping up to be the most important night of my life, Savvy. Gotta get it right."

"Hayden," she murmured.

I shook my head. "Nope. Not yet." I pointed to her mostly empty plate. "Eat. You can't dance on an empty stomach."

She nodded, quickly filling her plate with a little bit of everything.

Dinner continued in much the same way; pleasant small talk, devoid of any substance as we stuffed our faces. It was the first time since our first night that there was any real tension between us.

I stood, reaching for her hand just as she slipped the last bite into her mouth and laid her fork on the plate.

Not waiting for an objection, I pulled her into my arms and began swaying.

"I'm too tired to dance tonight."

"Savvy, we need to talk."

"I-I know. You said that if food and dancing don't work, we could go upstairs." She purred, dragging her finger down my chest, her eyes flicking up to meet mine. "Let's go. Convince me, handsome."

I stood still, my heart hammering against my ribcage, my body desperate to fulfill her commands. Still, my brain- "only if you promise to finish this in the morning."

I blew out a heavy breath. Of course I loved her body, but I hated conceding, leaving our future unsettled. But if it made her happy, I guess I could put it off, just for tonight.

Her hand slid down my arm, twining our fingers, pulling me gently toward the stairs and I followed willingly. Hell, I would follow this woman anywhere.

As we stepped into the small loft bedroom at the top of the stairs, I spun her around to face me, crashing my lips down on hers. She wanted convincing, I would give it to her.

She squirmed out of my hold. "Mmm, no. Not yet. God, Hayden, I feel sweaty and gross." She said, her mouth hanging open as a shiver worked its way down her spine.

"I can fix that." I whispered, scooping her up into my arms and stalking toward the bathroom, her answering laughter ricocheted off every solid surface, banishing the tension that had been present since she came through the front door tonight.

I flipped on the shower, spun the knob without looking, and turned to find her already nearly naked.

I pressed my lips to hers, a growl of appreciation rumbling in my chest as I watched her clothes drop to the floor piece by piece, my own clothes quickly following.

Our lips met in a fiery kiss as we stepped beneath the heated spray.

My hands cupped her face, pouring every drop of desire into her as we explored each other's mouths.

Her fingertips ghosted lightly over my chest and arms, moving in wide circles, her thumb nail rubbing gently across my nipples, earning her a soft hiss with every pass.

She shivered as my hands slid over the flat planes of her stomach, pushing up to cup her luscious breasts, giving her nipples a gentle squeeze.

Before she could react, before she made her move in our game of tit for tat, I dropped to my knees, lifted her leg over my shoulder and licked her from the bottom to the top, flicking my tongue over her clit a few extra times for good measure.

"Hayden!" she cried out, my name something between a prayer and a command, both hands sinking into my hair, pushing me closer to where she needed me.

I pushed a finger in, the slow languid strokes a sharp contrast to the frantic pace I kept with my tongue.

"Please. Please," she whispered, her voice nearly as shaky as her thighs.

"Hayden—I-I'm gonna fall,' she choked out." She choked out.

"I got you, Savvy. I won't let you fall."

"Uh- Oh- Oh God, Hayden!" she cried out, her legs giving way as her pleasure washed over her.

I held her against the wall, steadying her for a moment before standing and pushing into her.

She cried out, her head thrashing as I worked myself in and out of her. Her overly sensitive pussy fluttering with each thrust as each new sensation overwhelmed her senses.

"That's it. Let me hear how good I make you feel." I groaned, nipping at her earlobe.

I pounded into her hard and fast, every stroke building the inferno higher, hotter. I wanted to slow down, take my time, properly worship her body, but I couldn't. My need for her, to feel her, to have her feel me, was so strong it was all I could think of. A biological imperative I was powerless to resist.

"Hayden" she choked out in a hoarse whisper, her nails digging into my shoulders.

"We're almost there, Savvy," I gritted out. "Come with me."

"O-Oh! O-Oh fuck! Fuck! Oh, Hayden!" she screamed as her release hit, her pussy clamping down on me, milking me for every drop.

I lowered her feet to the floor and pressed a lingering kiss to her lips.

"Fuck, Savvy, you were perfect," I whispered against her hair.

I helped her wash her hair and spent a few minutes working out the knots in her back and thighs, my slippery soapy hands sliding easily against her wet body.

A quick half-assed towel dry and I carried her back to the bedroom, tossing her onto the bed and crawling over her.

"I don't intend for either of us to get much sleep tonight," I whispered as I settled myself between her legs.

She smiled softly, her fingertip tracing over my lips and down the column of my throat as I spoke.

"Sleep. Now where's the fun in that?" she giggled.

"My thoughts exactly." I answered, lowering my lips to hers in a deep passionate kiss as I pushed back into her.

Tonight, my need for her was insatiable, every cell alight, burning with an aching need only she could satisfy. Every kiss, every touch, felt like a promise—one I wasn't sure I had the right to make, but I would damn well keep if she let me.

Something deep and primal rumbled just beneath the surface, fed by her screams of pleasure, and I planned to spend from now until sunrise pulling every whimper, moan and scream I could manage from her exquisite body.

"Convince me," she said, well she didn't have a clue what kind of beast she unleashed with those words.

Chapter 14

SAVANNAH

Hayden had fallen asleep nearly two hours ago. I should have been sleeping too, but I wasn't. Instead, I was lying here with my head on his chest, drawing lazy circles with my fingertips and listening to his heartbeat as I contemplated my next move.

I loved Hayden, there was no denying it. Even though, just a week ago, I would have denied it without hesitation.

He spent nearly all our week together trying to bridge the gap between us, rebuild what we had. Anyone could see that—anyone, even someone as blind as I had been.

My mind kept pulling me down a spiral of 'what ifs,' tempting me to imagine alternate versions of the life we could have had.. What if Hayden and I had ended up together all those years ago? What if we had gotten married? What if he was the father of my children instead of- Nope, that was a bridge too far.

As much as I loved Hayden, Derek had been a good man and a loving husband. He didn't deserve to be pushed out of the place he held in my heart by a traitorous rewriting of history. My boys deserved more for their father's memory.

I pulled in a slow breath, pushing it out through barely parted lips. One breath and then another as I worked to redirect my errant thoughts and calm my raging heart.

Hayden and I had spent all our time talking about the past—about us. We hadn't even spoken about children, mine or his, though I had a feeling if he had children, they would have come with their father for Jude's funeral.

I slowly pushed myself up, instantly colder without the warmth of his body. My heart clenched as I realized I had already made my choice. I didn't need to wait until morning, and I certainly didn't need to hear some version of 'I don't want you' when he realized that raising another man's kids was part of the package.

My boys and I were a package deal, no exceptions. There wouldn't be any ignoring the kids and banging mom on the side. My life didn't have any room for 'I love you, but'.

He and Derek obviously hated each other. The one thought that kept racing through my mind was that the last time he had to choose, he chose to let me go.

If I was being perfectly honest with myself, I wouldn't have been strong enough to survive his rejection again. Maybe a week ago, but now... Now, after having him worship my body and whisper those three little words I waited most of my life to hear; I simply wasn't strong enough.

I slid out of bed, my feet silent on the hardwood as I hurried around the loft. I grabbed the clothing I had carelessly discarded over the past few days, a consequence of my brief, passion-fueled lapse in sanity.

I stuffed everything I could find into my suitcase, not caring that I was mixing clean with dirty. Cords, shoes, and my toothbrush, all found themselves stuffed into whatever pocket, bag, or case had enough space. I could sort it all out when I got home. For now, I had to get out of here as quietly as possible.

A coward. I knew that's what leaving in the dead of night, running away from Hayden and the conversation I promised him made me. Well, fine, I was a coward. Better that than the broken mess I would be after our conversation in the morning.

I thought of leaving a note, but what the hell was I supposed to say? *"Thanks for the sweet words and a good fuck, but it wouldn't have worked between us."*

Nothing I could scrawl on a tiny piece of paper would make this right and even attempting would take me all night.

My body shuddered as I closed the door behind me for the last time, each step beyond the door cutting into me like stepping on shards of shattered glass. The weight of each footstep drove them deeper until they were impossible to remove.

My laptop bag slipped from my shoulder, the sharp yank on my arm nearly caused me to drop my suitcase. I wanted to scream, to wallow in how bitterly unfair this moment was, but I couldn't, so I swallowed every bit of it and reminded myself this was my choice.

My chest tightened as I slid behind the wheel. The magnetic force that pulled me to him since we were children tugged so hard, I swore my heart might leap out of my chest and fly back to him.; I didn't blame it.

With trembling fingers, I turned the key, and backed down the driveway, holding my breath the entire twelve-minute drive to the interstate. As I merged onto the freeway, I released my captive breath and a torrent of bitter tears with it.

I crawled into bed just before nine. Too tired to move another inch and as much as I had missed them, I was grateful my boys were still sleeping.

I cried most of the four hours and thirty-eight-minute drive home. I had only managed to get the tears under control in the last half hour or so, mainly because I cried them all out.

My thoughts were still swirling too fast for me to catch onto them; to put them into neat little boxes and tuck them away. Hopefully after a few hours of sleep I would be able to do just that and move on from this week.

Who was I kidding? Even in the quiet recesses of my own mind I couldn't convince myself of that.

Even after I separated these memories and grieved the loss of what might have been, there would always be a deep permanent gash through the middle of my soul. That part of me would never be whole again, not without him.

Fat beams of sunlight fell across the bed, warming my face. I blinked a few times trying to orient myself. Home. This was home.

I reached under my pillow and pulled out my phone, one-thirty. "Shit!" I swore, shooting straight up.

I scrubbed my hands down my face and ran them through my tangled hair, trying to smooth myself out a bit, deciding after a minute or two, that was as good as it was going to get.

I slapped on a smile and opened the door.

Max and Chase were sitting on the sofa quietly playing video games but leaped from the sofa and ran to me as soon as they saw me.

"Hey Mom. How was your trip?" Max asked, his calm steady voice that echoed his father's, twisted something deep inside me.

Chase wrapped both arms around me, his large frame nearly swallowing me whole. "We missed you so much."

"Aww baby, I missed you too." I murmured, caressing his cheek, trying to remember when my baby boy got to be so grown up.

"My trip was fine. Thank you for asking." I replied to Max.

"We saw you were sleeping and figured you were tired from your trip, so we left you alone." Chase stumbled out.

"Thank you. I really needed the sleep." I answered truthfully. "But now I am starving."

"Can we order pizza?" Max piped up.

My stomach twisted at the memory of eating pizza naked in Hayden's arms. I think it would probably be a while before I could stomach the thought of that one.

"How about Chinese?" I suggested.

To my relief they both nodded eagerly. I pulled out my phone and punched out a delivery order for the Chinese place three blocks away. They had the best spring rolls in town and the boys always fought over who got the last one. I ordered extra, just in case.

The boys insisted I sit on the sofa and prop my feet up while they unloaded the car, even starting a load of my clothes in the washer for me.

I knew this wouldn't last, so I intended to soak up every second of this newfound appreciation my kids had for me. As I watched them crisscross back and forth, occasionally taking jabs at each other, I smiled, they were good kids, and I was lucky to be their momma.

After lunch, I had one lingering loose end to tie up from my week away. I needed to call Mr. Calder and see if he could refund me half what I paid. The cheeky bastard got paid twice, and he still hadn't refunded either of us. I figure if each of us paid half, it would be fair.

A quiet knock at the door pulled me from my thoughts. Chase was upstairs and Max was in the laundry room. I doubt either of them even heard the door.

"I'll get it," I called out.

I grabbed my debit card, my socked feet sliding across the tile floor with every step.

I yanked the door open, smiling at the absurdity of me nearly falling three times between the sofa and the door. What the hell did those boys mop with?

My smile froze halfway as my breath hitched in my chest. Standing on my porch, Hayden's green eyes—usually so vibrant—looked dull, his trademark smile nowhere in sight. My stomach twisted painfully at the sight of him.

"What are you doing here?" I asked, stepping onto the front porch and closing the door behind me.

"Hey Savvy." He responded quietly, his hands shoved down in the front pockets of his jeans. "You missed breakfast."

I stared back blankly, completely at a loss for how to answer him.

"How did you know where I live?" I blurted out the first thing that came to mind.

"Oh. That. Well, I sorta talked to Mr. Calder's daughter. She's nice. I explained the situation, and I asked her to refund your payment."

I opened my mouth to respond, but my lips refused to do much more than quiver before snapping shut again. "I-I don't–"

"She said she's a hopeless romantic and a sucker for a happy ending. She's rooting for us." He finished, offering me a sad smile.

"I'm a mom." I blurted out, then continued more calmly. "Two boys. Max and Chase."

He nodded. "I know."

"You knew?"

He shrugged. "Well, yeah. I mean, you two were married for a long time and... Fuck, Jude's best friend's cousin worked with Derek. Jude used to try to keep me updated on your life."

I nodded, again feeling lost for words.

"After a while, hearing tales of your happy life was a bit too much to bear. You were happy, I didn't need to know more. But yeah, I knew you two had a couple of kids. What of it?"

Now I felt really stupid. But just because he knew, didn't mean it actually changed the math. Then again, he was here...

"Look Hayden, I-" fuck, why was this so hard? "I realized we never had the *kids* conversation."

I scrubbed my hands down my thighs, drying my sweaty palms. "I-I don't know how to say this."

"Just spit the words out, Savvy. We can rearrange them until we understand each other, just get them out." He said, his voice softening.

"It all boils down to me not feeling right asking you to raise kids that aren't yours. I'm a mom Hayden, we're a package deal, my kids and me."

"Why would I have a problem with your kids?" he asked, his tone devoid of judgment like always.

"Because they aren't just mine, they are Derek's too. And you two hated each other."

A smile broke across his face, pulling a soft chuckle from him. "We didn't hate each other, Savvy. Derek was a good man, but we were rivals, and he won."

"That simple." I said, folding my arms across my chest.

"Not everything has to be complicated." He said, taking a cautious step closer.

"I want you. Now if that includes two kids, that's fine. If it includes six kids, two goats and a one-eyed dog, then that's fine too. As long as I can be with you."

I couldn't help the smile that bloomed on my face at his silly declaration, the humor instantly draining some of the tension away.

"So, you want to date a single mom, Hayden? Is that it?" I asked, looking away and tucking my messy curls behind my ear. Still afraid to see the answer in his eyes.

He hooked his finger under my chin and tipped it up to meet his gaze.

"No, Savvy. I don't want to date you."

My heart froze, desperate to avoid every painful beat that was coming.

"Dating is for getting to know each other. You know, kicking the tires a little and seeing if two people are compatible. We already know each other and if this past week is proof of anything it's that we are still very compatible."

I turned away, my cheeks heating as I hummed my agreement.

"I want to marry you, Savvy." His voice trembled slightly, and my heart twisted at the raw emotion in his words. "I know you probably still have some mixed feelings about me and Derek and all the history between us." He paused, swallowing hard, his Adam's apple bobbing as his gaze held mine. "Take your time but know this—that's my goal. You're it for me."

"I love you Savannah," he said, his voice breaking on my name. "And I can't think of anything more beautiful than for you to wear my ring and share my name."

The tears fell unbidden, neither of us trying to hold them back.

"Will you give me a chance to prove to you I'm worthy?" he asked, his brows crinkled and his whole body stiffened as if bracing for a painful impact.

I couldn't find words for this moment, so I just nodded, flashing him the biggest smile I could find, my arms wrapping around his neck and pulling him in for a deep, tender kiss, both of us pouring our all into that kiss.

"I love you, Hayden." I finally managed.

His answering smile was the most beautiful thing I had ever seen.

"I love you too, Savvy."

I laced our fingers and took a deep breath. "Then I guess there are two people you should meet." I said.

Hayden was right, this was simple.

I was the one letting fear whisper its bullshit into my ear and believing it. The entire drive home I felt sick to my stomach, like my body was rebelling against the thought of leaving him. But the thing about fear, it's a liar. Every. Single. Time.

Even now, taking the smallest of steps forward with Hayden felt right, with every cell in my body celebrating. I'm not saying my gut was always right, but I was willing to take a chance on it.

Just this one time.

Bonds of Blood and Soul

For nearly four centuries, Jackson has lived for himself and no one else. Unattached, unbothered, and perfectly content—until he meets her.

Valorey is everything he never wanted in amate. Beautiful, captivating, and seemingly perfect, with her dark eyes and a soul that calls to his. But there's one problem: Jackson has no intention of ever bonding with anyone. And Valorey—despite their undeniable connection—has a dangerous addiction that threatens to destroy them both.

Desperate to save her, Jackson turns toVerity, Valorey's twin sister, for help. Together, they embark on a mission to pull Valorey from the brink of self-destruction. But Jackson is hiding a dark secret: if his mate dies, the grief will push him beyond the point of no return, spiraling him into a feral rage with only one cure—death.

As love, sacrifice, and the battle against inner demons collide, Jackson must decide how far he's willing to go to save the woman who could be his undoing.

Bonds of Blood and Soul is a haunting and emotional tale of love that tests the limits of both heart and soul.
https://www.amazon.com/dp/B0DKBC9T3B

<u>Ignited</u>

Kendra is a fire mage living a quiet life. Until she crosses paths with a demon prince on a quest torule the seven realms. She suffers a devastating loss which puts her in a precarious position, between the demon and the thing he desires most.
Can she keep him from finding what he needs to fulfill the prophecy? Only time will tell...

https://www.amazon.com/dp/B0CMPQ6CF3

<u>Twin Flame</u>

Romantasy/FoundFamily/Fated Mates/Prophecy/Hidden Identity
Liam Bane has spent morethan 2300 years looking for his mate, his twin flame. He has traveled all over the seven realms only to find her in Everly, a fiery human girl at a bar three miles from home. There's just one problem with that. According to the law set down by the gods, humans can't be mated to dragons. Ever.
Now they must unlock the secrets of Everly's past as they fend off attacks from dragon slayers. allwhile working to fulfill an ancient prophecy that will save the seven realms from destruction.

https://www.amazon.com/gp/product/B0CGMFN84R

Triad of Souls
Hearts of Fire: Book 2

Finn and Marina set out to find the Scale of the GoldenDame. An
ancient artifact, lost to time. With few clues and only rumors and
whispers to follow, they must track down the scale before Farak, the
demon prince bent on dominating the seven realms, can find it.
They fight kidnappers, goblins, demons and more. But Finn's tough-
est battle may just be the redheaded mermaid traveling with him, his
mate, Marina.
The wayward mates must put aside their animosity to search for the
scale as well as the pieces of the Triad of Souls.
They say the man who wields the triad controls the world.Who will
find it first?
https://www.amazon.com/Triad-Souls-Hearts-Fire-Book-ebook/dp/
B0CS1ZNTDB

The Bite BeforeChristmas. A Vampire/Fae romance

No time of the year was worse than Christmas for Quinn Russell. He would almost rather go without both blood and sex, but as a vampire, he needed both. With everyone busy with the holiday, his only prospects were either lonely, desperate, or suicidal. A freak snowstorm causing a city wide blackout and leaves Quinn trapped in an elevator with a beautiful woman the Friday before Christmas. She's flawless. She's fae. And she just might be his mate.

https://www.amazon.com/dp/B0BMGVT9GM

Acknowledgements

This book would not have been written (probably) without Stephanie Swann being just as excited to read it as I was to write it! I can't say thank you enough. Your constant encouragement, wondering what Hayden and Savvy are up to, really pushed me when I needed it.

Louise. I am forever grateful you agreed to take a closer look and dive deep into the story. Your observations and perspective on their grief and how they would relate to each other helped me see it more clearly too. You also helped me find moments they could connect more deeply.

My beta readers are in fact the best. (Sorry other authors, mine ROCK!) I want to give a giant thank you to these amazing ladies who just let me drop my new book on them whenever I wish and they take their time to read it. Truly grateful.

Tiffany Eckmeyer
Tiffany Childs
Jennifer Parker
Jenn Elmer
Melissa Foerster
Barb Buchanan

And finally, I have to shout out to my husband and kids who have been overwhelmingly supportive of my writing. They have put up with late nights and distracted dinners as I have worked tirelessly to write this story while also writing two other books simultaneously. It has been an absolute marathon and I can't even begin to tell you how grateful I am for your support. I love you.

www.ingramcontent.com/pod-product-compliance
Lightning Source LLC
Chambersburg PA
CBHW060506300726
48975CB00008B/2671